A Book Of

EVENT MANAGEMENT

For

BBA Semester - VI

As Per New Syllabus w.e.f. 2015

Dr. HOSHI BHIWANDIWALLA
M.Com., D.H.E., D.M.S., Ph.D

BHAVANA CHAUDHARI
B.E. Electronics, M.B.A., B.C.J.

ADVANCEMENT OF KNOWLEDGE

N3463

Event Management (BBA - VI)

ISBN 978-93-5164-837-6

Second Edition : January 2017

© : Authors

Published By :
NIRALI PRAKASHAN
Abhyudaya Pragati, 1312, Shivaji Nagar,
Off J.M. Road, PUNE – 411005
Tel - (020) 25512336/37/39, Fax - (020) 25511379
Email : niralipune@pragationline.com

DISTRIBUTION CENTRES

PUNE

Nirali Prakashan : 119, Budhwar Peth, Jogeshwari Mandir Lane, Pune 411002, Maharashtra
Tel : (020) 2445 2044, 66022708, Fax : (020) 2445 1538
Email : bookorder@pragationline.com, niralilocal@pragationline.com

Nirali Prakashan : S. No. 28/27, Dhyari, Near Pari Company, Pune 411041
Tel : (020) 24690204 Fax : (020) 24690316
Email : dhyari@pragationline.com, bookorder@pragationline.com

MUMBAI

Nirali Prakashan : 385, S.V.P. Road, Rasdhara Co-op. Hsg. Society Ltd.,
Girgaum, Mumbai 400004, Maharashtra
Tel : (022) 2385 6339 / 2386 9976, Fax : (022) 2386 9976
Email : niralimumbai@pragationline.com

DISTRIBUTION BRANCHES

JALGAON

Nirali Prakashan : 34, V. V. Golani Market, Navi Peth, Jalgaon 425001,
Maharashtra, Tel : (0257) 222 0395, Mob : 94234 91860

KOLHAPUR

Nirali Prakashan : New Mahadvar Road, Kedar Plaza, 1st Floor Opp. IDBI Bank
Kolhapur 416 012, Maharashtra. Mob : 9850046155

NAGPUR

Pratibha Book Distributors : Above Maratha Mandir, Shop No. 3, First Floor,
Rani Jhanshi Square, Sitabuldi, Nagpur 440012, Maharashtra
Tel : (0712) 254 7129

DELHI

Nirali Prakashan : 4593/21, Basement, Aggarwal Lane 15, Ansari Road, Daryaganj
Near Times of India Building, New Delhi 110002
Mob : 08505972553

BENGALURU

Pragati Book House : House No. 1, Sanjeevappa Lane, Avenue Road Cross,
Opp. Rice Church, Bengaluru – 560002.
Tel : (080) 64513344, 64513355,Mob : 9880582331, 9845021552
Email:bharatsavla@yahoo.com

CHENNAI

Pragati Books : 9/1, Montieth Road, Behind Taas Mahal, Egmore,
Chennai 600008 Tamil Nadu, Tel : (044) 6518 3535,
Mob : 94440 01782 / 98450 21552 / 98805 82331,
Email : bharatsavla@yahoo.com

niralipune@pragationline.com | www.pragationline.com

Also find us on [f] www.facebook.com/niralibooks

Contents ...

Chapter 1...

Introduction to Event and Event Management

Contents ...

Learning Objectives ...

After going through this chapter, you will be able to gain an insight into the following

- To understand the meaning of events and the 5 C's of events.

- To learn the concept of event designing, event management and event marketing

- To study about the crucial 5 W's in organizing an event.

- To explain the different types and categories of events.

- To be aware of the problems associated with traditional media.

1.1   EVENT

1.1.1 Introduction

An Event is basically a phenomenon, any observable occurrence, or an extraordinary occurrence. It may be a type of **gathering,** a ceremony like a marriage, a convention (meeting), a happening, a performance or situation meant to be considered as art, a festival like a musical event, a media event, a happening that attracts coverage by mass media, a party, or a sporting event.

In **science, technology, and mathematics** a computing event may be a software message indicating that something has happened, such as a keystroke or mouse click; a relativity event may be a point in space at an instant in time, i.e. a location in space-time; a celestial event may be an astronomical phenomenon of interest.

In **philosophy**, an event may be an object in time, or an instantiation (the creation of an instance) of a property in an object; a mental event may be something that happens in the mind, such as a thought.

In **film, television and theatre**, the event may be a TV series, Veer Shivaji television series for Color TV channel; or a 2009 film Three Idiots directed by Vidhu Vinod Chopra.

An event in its universal and literal form would be something that takes place or happens or something needs to be done to organise the same. It is a significant occurrence or happening. It may be a social gathering/ activity or the outcome/ final result. In sports, an event is a contest or an item in a sports programme.

India has roughly 5000 fairs and festivals. This represents the biggest organised effort in events from ancient times. Originated on religious lines, these *melas* – which literally mean fairs – have always been a meeting ground for big and small traders, across the Indian subcontinent. Traditional games and entertainment have always been a part of such events. With their visually spectacular depiction of epic themes interwoven with singing, dancing and emoting, the events such as Indian fairs and festivals were a means of expression of the spiritual and cultural tradition of a community.

It is only a recent *avatar* as a marketing medium that events are attracting corporate attention and at the same time getting corporative itself. Rural India comprises over 75,000 villages and the TV penetration barely crosses 11% and the Internet effect is quite small. Therefore, to obtain reach for their communication campaigns, various corporates have resorted to events as a strategic alternative. Events have proved to be a versatile marketing communication tool since they can be easily customised to cater to the communication needs of the industry, whatever type it may be, as it integrates three traditional methods of marketing communication, viz. advertising, sales promotion and public relations.

1.1.2 Definition of Event

➤ **Philip Kotler**, the Marketing Guru, defines events as occurrences designed to communicate particular messages to target audiences.

➤ **Suresh Pillai**, Managing Director of Eventus Management, considers events as an additional media whereby two-way or active communication is possible.

➤ **Deepak Gattani**, Director, Unirapport Events, defines events as something noteworthy which happens according to a set plan involving networking of a multimedia package, thereby achieving the client's objectives and justifying their need for associating with events.

➤ **Professor Donald Getz** (1997), a well-known writer in the field of event management, defines special events from two perspectives, that of the customer and that of the event manager, as follows:

  • A special event is a one-time or infrequently occurring event outside normal programmes or activities of the sponsoring or organising body.

  • To the customer or guest, a special event is an opportunity for leisure, social or cultural experience outside the normal range of choices or beyond everyday experience.

➤ Another well-known author, **Dr. J. Goldblatt** (1997), defines special events as "a unique moment in time celebrated with ceremony and ritual to satisfy specific needs."

1.1.3 A Comprehensive New Definition

A key component existing within nearly every organisation regardless of industry, country or otherwise is the notion of an 'event'. Some may call this a message, indicator, notification or something similar. Events simply communicate a message to something. The message communicated can be good, bad or indifferent, true or false, on or off, verbose or terse. The something on the receiving end of an event can be a human, system, or other application, code or similar logic. Events form the basis and are the conveyance mechanism of choice. The events are characterised by the following:

> ➢ They are often "once in a lifetime" experiences for the participants.
>
> ➢ They are generally expensive to stage.
>
> ➢ They usually take place over a short time span.
>
> ➢ They require long and careful planning.
>
> ➢ They generally take place only once. However, many are held annually, usually, at the same time every year.
>
> ➢ They carry a high level of risk, including financial risk and safety risk.
>
> ➢ There is often a lot at stake for those involved, including the event management team.

An event can be described as a public assembly for the purpose of celebration, education, marketing or reunion. It is a different way of promoting a product, service or idea. An event is the successful implementation of a vision. An event is used as a very powerful promotional tool to launch or market a product or service by managing it efficiently and effectively.

Figure 1.1 is a diagrammatical representation which illustrates the comprehensive definition of an event. It is evident from the model that an event is a package so organised as to provide reach and live interaction between the target audience and the client to achieve the desired impact. The event is exposed to the population of the target audience called the reach for the event. The live interaction process facilitates communication between the clients and the audience. This process strengthens the possibilities of mutually beneficial transactions occurring in tune with the desired objectives for the event.

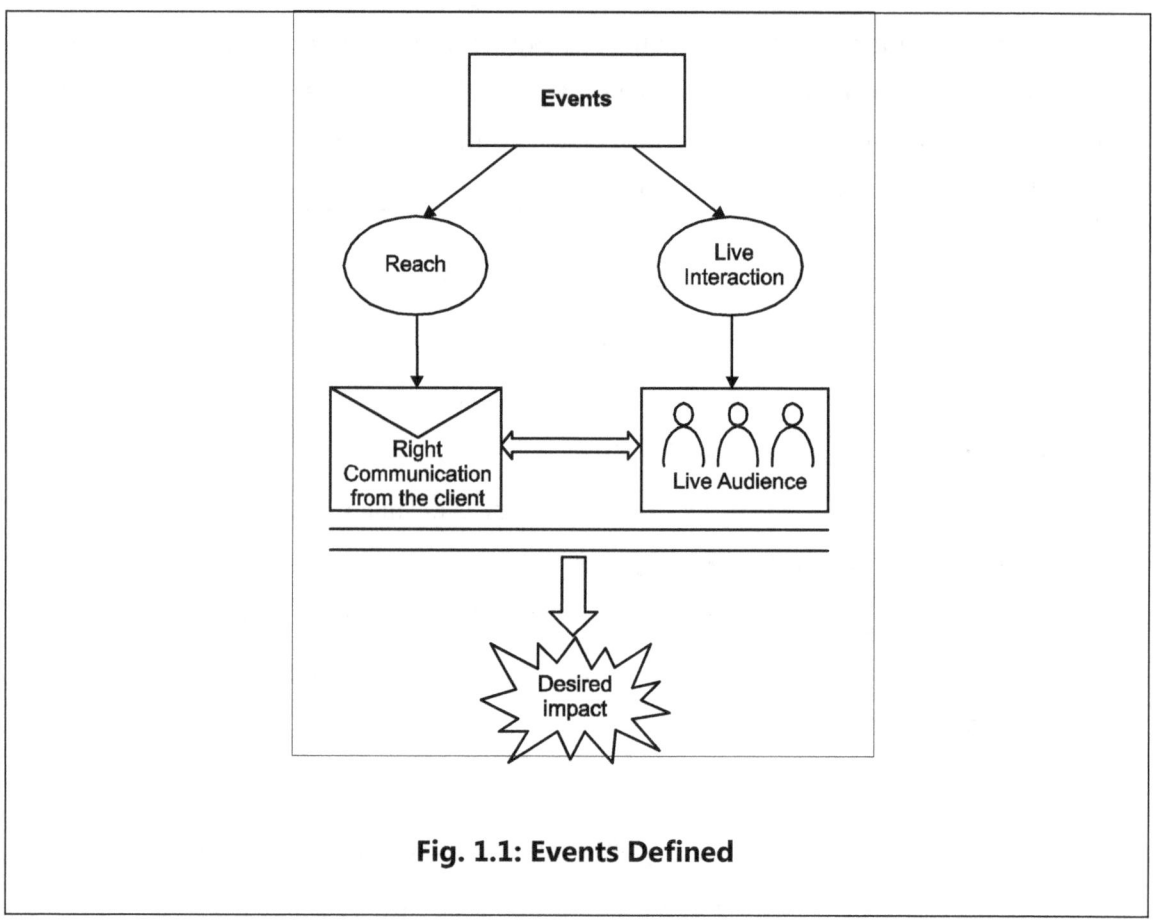

Fig. 1.1: Events Defined

An event is a live multimedia package carried out with a preconceived concept, customised or modified to achieve the clients objectives of reaching out and suitably influencing the sharply defined, specially gathered target audience by providing a complete sensual experience and an avenue for two-way interaction. An event is the successful implementation of a vision.

1.1.4 Event Management

Many of us have observed events, most of us have participated in events, but few of us have managed events. Event management is the planning and management of an event, project or activity. Managing an event means ensuring the smooth running of the event, by minimising the risks and maximising the enjoyment of the event audience.

Event management is defined as the science of managing events. Event management is the application of project management to the creation and development of festivals, events and conferences. Event management is the process by which an event is planned, prepared and produced. As with any other form of management, it encompasses all the activities involved in assessment, definition, acquisition, allocation, direction, control and analysis of time, finances, people, products, services, and other resources to achieve objectives. Event management involves studying the intricacies of the brand, identifying the target audience, devising the event concept, planning the logistics and coordinating the technical aspects before actually executing the modalities of the proposed event. Post-event analysis and ensuring a return on investment have become significant drivers for the same.

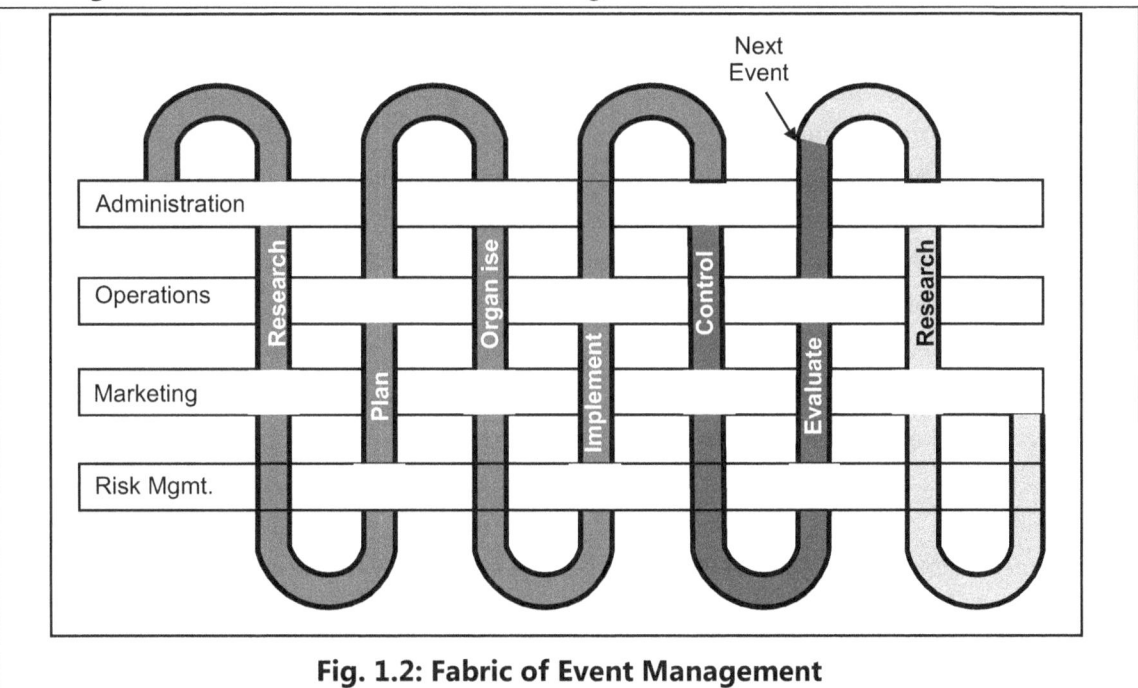

Fig. 1.2: Fabric of Event Management

Event management is an intricate weaving of the process and the scope of management functions. The functional units form the warp fibres – the foundation threads of the fabric of an event. The processes - or weft threads – are interwoven through these foundations for each event, with the evaluation thread from one event forming the research thread for the next event. If one of the threads is eliminated, the fabric of the event is weakened, leaving holes or places where it may unravel.

All operational tasks for an event such as the ground work, venue selection, stage design, arranging the infrastructure facilities required, liaison with artists or performers and networking with other activities such as advertising, PR, ticket sales, etc. fall under the purview of event management. Today event management is emerging as a top industry, growing at the rate of 250% and proving to be a very lucrative and rewarding career.

The event manager brings an event to reality by a skilful blend of ideas, creativity, logistics, budgets, permits, people, performers, the publicity channels, the market, and organising of all these and the end result is a successful event – A FULFILLED VISION. An event manager has to be a jack of all and a master of blending all skills like planning, organising abilities, promotion, motivating people and a touch of classy creativity to unfold a grand event in front of the audience where there are no retakes.

1.1.5 Event Marketing

Nothing happens until somebody sells something. Nowhere is it truer than in the event industry. While marketing an event, the marketing process must begin at the outset of the planning process, during the setting of the goals and objectives of the event itself. Marketing must both reflect and drive those objectives. It must also integrate those into one goal and enlist people into action toward the fulfillment of that goal. Marketing can play a vital role in the "search and discover" effort to identify new markets in which to promote an event. And of course, it should include all the other classic elements of marketing, such as advertising, telemarketing, and promotional campaigns, to bring all of the event goals to life.

Event marketing involves canvassing for clients and arranging feedback for the creative concepts during and after the concept initiation so as to arrive at a customised package for the client, keeping the brand values and target audience in mind. Event management experts have defined event marketing in a variety of ways.

➢ Event marketing is a state of focused event strategy managed consistently over a period of time to reinforce aspects of brand character.

➢ Event marketing is a rifle shot approach to one's audience where there is very little wastage.

➢ Event marketing includes promotional activities involving an event such as a sporting or social event, designed to bring a product to the attention of the public.

➢ The marketing discipline focused on face to face interaction via live events, trade shows and corporate meetings among other event types. Event Marketing covers business to business (B2B), business to consumer (B2C), and business to Government (B2G) marketing. Differing from traditional marketing such as print, radio and television, event marketing takes into consideration all of the aspects of a live experience including, spatial design, graphic design, video, audio, web, interactive and live talent to create a motivating and memorable experience.

Ideally, event marketing involves simultaneous canvassing and studying the brand prints, understanding what the brand stands for, it's positioning and values, identifying the target audience and liaisoning with the creative conceptualisers to create an event for a perfect mesh with the brand's personality.

1.1.6 Five C's of Events

The activities required for marketing and managing events require certain steps to be followed that can be called the 5 C's of events.

Conceptualisation of the creative idea or ambience,

Costing i.e. calculation of cost of production and margins on the event,

Canvassing for clients, sponsors, customers or audience and networking components,

Customisation of the concept depending on the customers' needs and marketing objectives,

Carrying-out the event i.e. execution of the event as planned which is most important part of event management.

1.1.7 Event Designing

In practice, each of the C's may not strictly adhere to the sequence in which they have been presented above. There is a complex interaction between the various C's before the carrying stage, depending on the requirements of the client, constraints forced by budgets, etc. The final concept, which is going to be actually carried out, is a derivative of a series of modifications to the initial concept. The final concept is arrived at after accommodating changes required for a perfect fit amongst all other C's during the conceptualisation process. This process can be termed as event designing.

In event designing, consistency and links to the purpose of the event are all essential parts of the creative process. The following are the main creative elements that must be considered.

1. **Theme:** The theme should ideally appeal to all senses – tactile, smell, and taste, visual and auditory. If the aim of the event is to create a unique and memorable experience for the audience, then appealing to all the senses will contribute positively to the outcome. Keep in mind that needs of the audience vary enormously.

2. **Layout:** This creative element which gives the feeling of socially comfortable feeling is so far given far too little consideration. Discomfort should not be the result of being in too much open or congested space, not enough light or too much of it, or having just a limited opportunity for people to mix. The audience needs to comfortably fill the venue to create a positive ambience.

3. **Decor:** Fabrics, decorative items, stage props, drapes, and table settings can all be rented. It is generally worthwhile investigating these options before deciding on the event theme, since renting items can reduce costs enormously. Floral arrangements need to be ordered from the experienced florists, as they provide a dramatic effect.

4. **Suppliers:** Good relationships with the suppliers of all the commodities will ensure the event organisers that only quality products will be received, including the freshest flowers and the best produce that the markets can supply. During most large events, suppliers are pressed for the best quality from all the customers at a time when volumes are much larger than usual. This is a situation in which a good long-standing relationship with a supplier is invaluable.

5. **Technical Requirements:** Problems caused by lack of technical back-up can be reduced by technical support. Technical glitches by the contracted company are unacceptable. Microphones must have back-ups, the power supply must be assured, and stages and video screens must be visible to all in the audience. There is no substitute for wide-ranging experience, and this is a key attribute that should be sought when choosing technical contractors. New technology, especially anything used to demonstrate new products, needs to be tested thoroughly, through many rehearsals. A backup system is essential.

6. **Entertainment:** Entertainment is central for some events, while for some events, it is peripheral. The most important thing is that the entertainment should suit the purpose of the event, not detract from it. The needs of the event audience must be carefully considered when making this decision.

7. **Catering:** Whereas guests may have patience with other delays, perhaps delays in service and poor quality, poor taste food make participants at an event very much frustrated.

1.1.8 5 W's in Organising an Event

To organise a good event you research on the FIVE crucial W's and involve one 'F'. The F is the Finance for preparing the budget. The crucial 5 W's are Why, What, Who, When and Where.

WHY do the Event? Is it for product sales (Product launches, Ad Campaign etc.), or celebrate a festival (Dandiya, Ganesh Ustav etc.) or enhancing Corporate image? (Femina, Filmfare, Screen etc.). These are just a few reasons.

Next is **WHAT** — what the Event is all about. Is it an award ceremony, exhibition, show, seminar, marriage, party.

WHO will do the Event? The company or do they engage an Event Manager? Today it is mostly the latter.

WHEN you do the Event is equally important. Could a college organise a Youth Festival in March/April (Exam time) or keep a Conference where people have to travel distances on the Ganpati Visarjan day? Definitely not.

WHERE you organise (the venue) is worth a thought. Say a Chartered Accountant's meet is best hosted in the evening at a Town Hall; would you keep Dandiyas too close to residential areas.

These Five W's are a test of the Event Manager's abilities and foresight.

THE FIVE W's = HOW TO PRODUCE CONSISTENTLY EFFECTIVE EVENTS

Too often students will ask "what event" they should produce for a class projects instead of "Why" they should produce the event in the first place. Following the economically unsteady early 1990s, corporations, associations, governments, and other organisations began to carefully analyse why a meeting or event should occur. This solid reasoning should be applied to every event decision.

The first step is to ask "Why" must we hold this event? There must be not one but a series of compelling reasons that confirm the importance and viability of holding the event.

The second step is to ask "Who" will be the stakeholders for this event? Remember stakeholders are both internal and external parties. Internal stakeholders may be your board of directors, committee members, staff, elected leaders, guests, or others. External stakeholders may be the media, politicians, bureaucrats, or others who will be investing in your event. Conducting solid research will help you determine the level of commitment of each of these parties and better help you decide "who" this event is being produced for.

The third step is to determine "When" this event is being held. You must ask yourself if the research through evaluation time frame is appropriate for the size of this event. If this window of time is not appropriate you may need to rethink your plans and either shift the dates or streamline your operations. "When may also determine where the event may be held."

The fourth step involves determining "Where" the event will be held. Once you have selected a site, as you will discover in this chapter, your work becomes either easier or more challenging. Therefore, this decision must be made as early as possible as it affects many other decisions.

The fifth and final "W" is to determine from the information gleaned thus far "What" is the event product you are developing and presenting matching the event product to the needs, wants, desires and expectations of your guests while satisfying the internal requirement of your organisation is no simple task. "What" must be carefully and critically analysed to make certain the why, who, when, and where are synergies in this answer.

Once these five questions have been thoroughly answered it is necessary to turn your attention to how we are to use SWOT analysis for it.

1.1.9 Types of Events

There are different ways of classifying and categorising events. Events are classified by size, form and type.

According to Brenda R. Carlos, events can be classified as:

(1) Sporting,

(2) Entertainment, Arts, and Culture,

(3) Commercial Marketing and Promotional Events,

(4) Meetings and Exhibitions,

(5) Festivals,

(6) Family,

(7) Fundraising, and

(8) Miscellaneous Events.

According to **National Institute of Event Management**, events in India can be classified as:

(1)   Hall Mark Events: i.e. an event related to a place, like the Delhi Asian games or the Sydney Olympics etc.

(2) **Celebrations:** includes festivals like Navratris, Ganesh Utsavs, Pongal, Baisakhi etc., Mega shows and Award Nights like Femina, Filmfare, Screen, Gladrags etc.

(3) **Concerts:** International artist shows like Elton John Concert, Bryan Adams Show, etc.

(4) **Educational Events:** like Seminars, Conferences, and Exhibitions etc.

(5) **Marketing Events:** leading to Promotions, Road shows, Ad Campaigns and Contests, Product launches etc.

(6) **Hospitality Events:** include Hotel events like Conferences, Food Festivals etc.

(7) **Others:** are Tourism events like Festivals of India, Huge sports events, retail events and contests etc.

Events can also be classified by type of activity or performance in it:

These include sporting, special events, entertainment, art and cultural, commercial, marketing and promotional events, and meetings, conventions and exhibitions.

1. **Sporting events** are those that attract sportsmen and women from the highest levels from all over the world, like the Olympic Games. Special events are classified as being unique and, for the client, "an opportunity for a leisure, social or cultural experience outside the normal range of choices or beyond everyday experience. "

2. **Special events** are those such as weddings. Festivals, including entertainment, cultural and arts, are usually community events and can attract any number of people from 50 to 500,000.

3. **Commercial, marketing and promotional events** tend to have high budgets and high profiles. Allen et al. explains that success is vital because the company wants to market their product to the consumer and differentiate it from its competitors.

As already explained an event can be described as a public assembly for the purpose of celebration, education, marketing or reunion.

Another classification of events can be:

1) **Social / Life–cycle events:** Events like Birthday party, Hen/Stag party, Graduation day, Bachelor's party, Engagement, Wedding, Anniversary, Retirement day, Funeral etc.

2) **Education and career events:** Events like education fair, job fair, workshop, seminar, debate, contest, competition etc.

3) **Sports events:** Events like Olympics, World Cup, Marathons, Wimbledon, wrestling matches etc.

4) **Entertainment events:** Events like music concerts, fairs, festivals, fashion shows, award functions, celebrity nights, beauty peagents, flash mob, jewellery shows, stage shows etc.

5) **Political events:** Events like political procession, demonstration, rally, political functions etc.

6) **Corporate events:** Events like MICE (meetings, incentives, conferences, exhibitions), product launches, road shows, buyer-seller meet etc.

7) **Religious events:** Events like religious festivals / fairs, religious procession, Katha, Pravachan, Diwali fair, Dusherra fair etc.

8) **Fund raising/ cause related events:** Any event can be turned into a fund raising or cause related event e.g. auctions.

1.1.10 Categories of Events (Also refer 2.1.5 for the details.)

Events can also be classified into four broad categories based on their purpose and objective.

1. Leisure events, e.g. Leisure sport, music, recreation.
2. Cultural events, e.g. ceremonial, religious, art, heritage and folklore.
3. Personal events, e.g. Weddings, birthdays, anniversaries.
4. Organisational events, e.g. commercial, political, charitable, sales, product launch, expo.

According to size, events may be categorised as:

1. **Mega Events:** The largest events are called mega events, which are generally targeted at international markets. The Olympics Games, The Wimbeldon series, World Cup Soccer, Maha Kumbh Mela are good examples. All such events have a specific yield in terms of increased tourism, media coverage, and economic impact. These events will generally have a much longer time span than other events, and can go on for several weeks.

Maha Kumbh Mela, which translated means the "Great Urn Fair", the largest religious gathering in history. In the 2001 event, approximately 70 million Hindu Pilgrims converged on the Ganges and Yamuna Rivers in Allahabad, India, for a sacred bathing ritual that devotees believe will purify and break the cycle of reincarnation. The gathering takes place every 12 years. The 2001 festival, described as the "Greatest Show on Earth", was arguably the largest gathering of humanity ever for a single event.

2. **Regional Events:** Regional events are designed to increase the appeal of a specific tourism destination or region. FAN Fair, the world's biggest country music festival, held annually in Nashville, Tennessee, Marathon, Mumbai, Asian Games.

3. **Major Events:** These events attract significant local interest and large number of participants, as well as generating significant tourism revenue. As an example, New Year Celebrations are held in most of the major cities. Most major cities have a convention centre capable of holding large meetings, trade shows and conventions. According to Allen et al. major events are classified as "attracting significant local interest and large number of participants". A consumer show aimed at the general public which includes subjects like home interiors, clothes, fashion etc. is an example of a major event.

4. **Minor Events:** Most events fall into this category and it is here that most managers gain their experience. Almost every town, city, country and state host various annual events like agricultural fairs and expos etc., held each year. In addition to annual events, there are many one-time events, including historical, cultural, musical, and dance performances. Meetings, parties, celebrations, conventions, award ceremonies, exhibitions, sporting events and many other community and social events come under this category.

In the next chapter, we will be studying about the core concept. The core concept is responsible for giving rise to event categories and delineating the basic differences amongst. We can classify events into six different categories with the help of these variations. It also covers some of the innumerable event variations that are possible during the event design process. The different bases such as time, location, value, concept, artist and client affect this process. Please refer to 2.1.5 Categories of events and its characteristics for more details.

1.1.11 Objectives of Event Management

Before we see the objectives of event management, just imagine and think why event. The purpose may be either and or. It may be Advertising, Launching, Promotion, Implementation of marketing plan, Focusing the target market, Relationship building, Brand building, and/or increasing sudden turn-over. As we have studied earlier, event management is the art and science of managing events. It is the process by which an event is planned, prepared and produced. As it encompasses all management activities, it makes us think that why a need of event management is there or what are its objectives.

1. To study the purpose of the event.

2. To devise the event concept.

3. To identify the target audience.

4. To study the intricacies of the brand.

5. To plan the logistics required.

6. To prepare the required budget.

7. Acquisition, allocation and optimum utilization of resources.

8. To coordinate the technical aspects before actual execution of modalities of the proposed event.

9. To ensure the return on investment.

10. To ensure about the disaster management system.

11. To design the feedback system and do post-event analysis.

1.1.12   Problems Associated with Traditional Media

The problems associated with traditional media that has been used for fulfilling marketing requirements are listed below

1. Too many advertisements have caused cluttering on TV, print and other media. This has generated a need for avenues that provide exclusivity to the sponsor while not sacrificing the advantages of reach and impact.

2. The growing number of TV channels and the greater number of programmes has caused disintegration of the viewership. Thus, there is a need for broadcasting campaigns to the target audience.

3. Rapid increase of low intensity television viewers who see a little of each channel causes a need to capture the full attention of the target audience.

4. Media cost inflation that is, because of rising inflation, which has been eroding the advertising budgets; advertisers are demanding the best return from every ad-rupee spent. Media planning has become more difficult and thus the need for increased effectiveness with regards to tangible impact that can be assessed immediately, has risen.

5. Rapid increase in the number of media channels, therefore the need for intelligent media buying.

Points to Remember

- An event in its universal and literal form would be something that takes place or happens or something needs to be done to organise the same.

- An event can be described as a public assembly for the purpose of celebration, education, marketing or reunion. It is a different way of promoting a product, service or idea.

- An event is a live multimedia package carried out with a preconceived concept, customised or modified to achieve the client's objectives of reaching out and suitably influencing the sharply defined, specially gathered target audience by providing a complete sensual experience and an avenue for two-way interaction.

- The five W's = Why, What, Who, When and Where.

- "What" must be carefully and critically analysed to make certain the why, who, when, and where are synergies in this answer.

- According to the size, events may be categorised as Mega Events, Regional Events, Major Events, and Minor events.

- Event management is the planning and management of an event, project or activity.

- Managing an event means ensuring the smooth running of the event, by minimising the risks and maximising the enjoyment of the event audience.

- While marketing an event, the marketing process must begin at the outset of the planning process, during the setting of the goals and objectives of the event itself.

- Ideally, event marketing involves simultaneous canvassing and studying the brand prints, understanding what the brand stands for, its positioning and values, identifying the target audience and liaison with the creative conceptualisers to create an event for a perfect mesh with the brand's personality.

- The activities required for marketing and managing events require certain steps to be followed – Conceptualisation, Costing, Canvassing, Customisation, and Carrying out - that can be called the 5 C's of events.

- In event designing, consistency and links to the purpose of the event are all essential parts of the creative process. The Theme, Layout, Decor, Suppliers, Technical Requirements, Entertainment and Catering are the main creative elements that must be considered.

Questions for Discussion

1. What do you mean by an 'event'? How is it defined?

2. Describe the 5 C's of events. How are those used in the event designing?

3. Explain how to organise and produce consistently effective events with the help of 5 W's.

4. How the events are classified and categorised?

5. What are the objectives of event management?

6. Enumerate and discuss the problems associated with the traditional media?

Chapter 2...

Facets of Event Management

Contents ...

Learning Objectives ...

After going through this chapter, you will be able to gain an insight into the following

- To understand event infrastructure and its essential elements.
- To learn how to negotiate contracts with event organisers.
- To know the key points on which event organisers should stress upon.
- To study the criteria for selection of a venue for the event.

2.1 EVENT INFRASTRUCTURE

Event infrastructure includes those essential elements without which there cannot be any event. These essential elements are core concept, core people, core talent, and core structure. The nature of this infrastructure varies with the event categories and variations in events.

2.1.1 Core Concept

"Core concept" is a term that defines the basic concept of an event and the various major categories of events. It is the first step to event infrastructure. The basic visualisation, designing and planning of the event is included in core concepts. It is a term that can be used to define the fundamental underlying ethos and evolution of the various major categories of events. An entire event family is based on event categories. These differences in event categories lead to innumerable variations in event. Therefore, the core concept of an event is like a root of a tree that generates the energy, lays down the base and the type of tree that shall grow.

2.1.2 Core People

Core people are the main people, that is, the organisers of the event. These main people are the people actually performing, acting or participating in the process of influencing the audience. They play an important role in influencing the audience to create a desired impact. This desired impact is in terms of a favourable position for the clients brand in the mind of the audience.

When the event gets underway, these are the people who hold way and take the centre stage. The audience comes to experience the expertise, charisma or knowledge of such core people and to have an opportunity to interact with them. The personality of the core people being used in an event should match the brand personality.

2.1.3 Core Talent

Core talent is the talent of the people performing, acting or participating in an event. That means, core talent is the talent of core people. Core people are required to have talents such as specific expertise, reputation and knowledge. It is the core talent of the core people that attracts and influences the audience. For example, in a music concert, the type of audience that will get attracted to this event depends on the talent of the performer. As mentioned before, an event family is based on event category. This core talent of the core people helps in creating variations in event categories. For example, in music there are different categories. The event can either be classical, pop, jazz, rock, etc. If it is an event of sports, the event differs in constraints of boundary. The physical manifestation of these constraints that acts as a challenge or obstacle varies from game to game. They lead to the need for different talents required in playing each game. Core talent is game specific in sports, that is, talent required for football differs from the talent required to play baseball and talent required for baseball differs from talent required to play basketball.

2.1.4 Core Structure

The presence of a formal or informal organisation to manage the event category as a whole is important to make it lucrative from its marketing point of view. Depending upon the degree to which the event category is structured the requirements of management and marketing of events may vary.

The more formal and structured it is, the more lucrative that event category becomes, since it becomes easier to manage and market. By more formal and structured, we mean that, there is a proper organisational structure in which roles and responsibilities are clearly assigned to different members of the organisation along with proper delegation of authority to carry out these roles. Depending on the stakes involved - not only in terms of money but also of national pride and identification of the event category by the ordinary citizens - each of the categories has become structured to certain degrees.

This organisation for efficient management has been denoted as the core structure. Traditionally, across the world, competitive events have always been comprehensively administered right from the grass root level, that is, right from the schools with league matches at every level up to the international level. In fact, competitive events are the only category among all categories of events that have a strong and structured organisation. Among competitive events, sporting events are the most organised and structured both nationally and internationally. Sports control bodies such as the BCCI (Board of Control for

Cricket in India) or ICC (International Cricket Council) are examples of this. Such bodies not only carry out managerial functions and other administrative activities involved with the event but also focus on the members and players benefits during, and to an extent, after their playing tenure.

A formal structure is not available for the other event categories, though informal arrangements do exist. Cause-based events are an example of events not having an organised structure since such events are usually one-off in nature and there is no organised body involved in arranging events for fund raising or creating awareness for the event category of the cause as a whole.

2.1.5 Categories of Events and its Characteristics

Variations in the core concepts distinguish the various categories of events. Based on this principle, events as a marketing tool can be broadly categorised as under:

A. Competitive Events.   B. Artistic Expression.

C. Cultural Celebrations.   D. Exhibition Events.

E. Charitable Events.   F. Special Business Events.

A. Competitive Events

Core concept: This involves a test of physical strength, mental ability and talent or a combination of these, it is a challenge between two or more entities whether individuals or a group of people from different communities. These individuals may be amateurs or professionals, a classy and controlled variation of crude warfare that involves patriotism, pain and pride in victory. An encounter simply with an aim to enjoy the clash of skills and the mastery of intricacies involved in the event by the members taking part.

Types of competitive events: Competitive events can be classified into different types. These are contests which test sporting skills, artistic talents, and knowledge levels or compare participants based on the parameter as a constraint within a specific set of rules and regulations applicable to all. The most visible examples of competitive events are sports, talent and beauty contests.

Characteristics: As competitive events are the most famous events category, they have tended to become mass audience-oriented. The opportunities to telecast live for the television media - and thereby increased scope for reach and revenue - has tended to blur, the interaction part of the benefit provided by events. Besides that, the excitement generated during such an event holds the spectators interest. Any communication redirecting their attention from the contest could be perceived as an intrusion. Thus, competitive events provide more reach and fewer interactions. Given these characteristics, competitive events are mainly used for:

- ➢ Visibility and exposure to the brands
- ➢ Prolonged impact
- ➢ Corporate/brand awareness
- ➢ Consolidating the positioning of brands
- ➢ Merchandising and sale of licensed products around the event.

The most famous competitive events are sporting events. The madness surrounding the 2000 Olympic Games held in Australia is an evidence of the popularity connected to sports so much that it is publicised as the best show on planet Earth. Games have always developed from the culture and lifestyles of the people. Changing daily activity by magnifying the constraints into a competition was a definite way to have fun and test people's courage and wisdom. If not each community, generally every country at least has a few games that have evolved locally.

The popularity of sporting events and its continuous effect can be judged by the re-launch in India of Prudential, an UK-based insurance firm. The Prudential World Cup of 1983 will forever remain etched in the minds of millions of cricket *aficionados* in India. Despite many difficulties, Kapil Dev, one of the world's greatest all-rounder and the Indian captain in the 1983 World Cup held in England and his team made India proud by winning the cup. They defeated the West Indies who had won all of the three previous World Cups. In the year 1983 when India won the world cup against West Indies, the whole country celebrated, which is unmatched till date. Exactly 15 years later, Prudential, which was pulled out of India because of some reasons, was on the front pages of leading Indian newspapers and in the reports on a large number of satellite channels. Why? The stars of 1983 – to be exact, the whole team was present at the launch ceremony where a replica of Prudential Cup was rewarded in a mock ceremony to Kapil Dev by a top-ranking official from Prudential. There was not a single advertisement released neither in newspapers nor on television. Yet, every cricket fan was aware of the re-entry of Prudential into India.

This is just a post-event benefit. There are many other benefits attached to the associated competitive events. They have a *prolonged impact* because one can built on a competitive event, have follow-ups, and feature a series for many weeks before and after the event. The sponsor can have curtain-raisers and curtain-downers, and therefore keep the event alive.

Still a new and exotic game for Indians, Bacardi Asian Beach Volleyball Championship on the Chowpatty beach in Mumbai fitted in completely with the brand image and publicity requirements of Bacardi, a liquor brand launched in India in late 90s. The reason for this interest in sports is because of widespread national and international television coverage thus providing visibility and exposure with the brands of the sponsoring companies at a comparatively low cost. In addition to the excitement is the prospect of live coverage providing greater value to the audience and a chance for a larger reach to the event.

The remarkable increase in popularity of competitive events for sponsorship can be credited to the introduction of satellite television. Moving beyond corporate/brand awareness, competitive events are also being used by companies for consolidating the positioning of brands in the minds of the consumers. For example, sponsoring sporting events such as golf, polo, tennis, squash, etc. is like marketing a lifestyle for rich influential audience. The 1996 Miss World pageant sponsored by Godrej with ABCL, handling the marketing and management of the show is another example that can be cited here. Coming as it were, after the crowning of Sushmita Sen and Aishwarya Rai as Miss Universe and Miss World respectively, it was a perfect chance for Godrej to strengthen its position as a world-class firm particularly, after the restructuring of its tie-up with Procter & Gamble.

Sports venues generally have many sponsors and branding opportunities surrounds the whole playing area. The boundaries especially are the main spots. Other unique branding opportunities exist in different games. In tennis, for example, the guts of the rackets of players carry the logo of the sponsors. It is the same on the dress or uniform that the players wear. The 1998 World Cup soccer tournament in France is the ultimate example of the sporting events with the sponsors. The total value of the 12 World Cup sponsors and the organising committee was about $ 428 million. Besides this, the turnover from the sales of the sale of World Cup licensed products was estimated at over $1 billion. And these figures do not include money by other advertisers. Other sponsors include those who have agreed to back World Cups teams or for providing services to the organisers or for television broadcasting rights.

The competitive spirit is not only limited to the sporting arena. When it comes to competition, creative minds and spirits equally share the limelight. De Beers, the World's biggest diamond mining firm, in collaboration with The Gem and Jewellery Export Promotion Council, organised a unique competition to celebrate the beginning of the new millennium----the premier Annual National Diamond Design Contest. The focus of the contest was the creative diamond jewellery designs that women would love to wear in the new Millennium. De Beers took special delight in inviting all designers to take part in a design competition that gave artists a great chance to display their talent on a scale like never before. It was undoubtedly a competition that offered talented designers a platform to show their talent on the world stage and to win national plus international recognition. Most significantly, the winning designers got a chance to be the creator of the Millennium Diamond Design and to attend The Diamond International Awards ceremony in Paris. At the event, also known as the Oscar's in Jewellery Awards, amongst 30 millennium winners, three Indian jewellery designers won the Diamond International Awards 2000. The presentation was during the Haute Couture week. The year 2000 competition broke all records for entries with 2530 designs submitted from 42 countries. The winners came from 17 countries: Australia, Belgium, Brazil, Canada, France, Germany, Hong Kong, India, Italy, Israel, Japan, Korea, Mexico, South Africa, United Arab Emirates, United Kingdom and United States of America. The post-event follow-up included an Indian Exhibition in October 2000 where the Indian audience also had an opportunity to see the newest talent as the Diamonds International Awards 2000 Collection was on a world tour after the awards presentation in Paris.

B. Artistic Expression

Core concept: The idea is to entertain the audience by showcasing the artist's talents. It may involve singing, dancing, theatre, etc. and is a form of expression of emotion and freedom.

Types of events for artistic expression: Music concerts, dance ballets and other stage performance are the most famous types of artistic expression. These are only for entertaining the audience.

Characteristics: Since entertainment is the only and main objective at such events, the audience dislikes any commercial interactions, though the client and event organiser may welcome significant interactions. Therefore, events for artistic expression give opportunity for more reach and fewer interactions because of which the major benefits that such event offers to potential sponsors are:

 ➢ Consolidation of the image of their brands.

 ➢ Post-event mileage.

 ➢ Excellent coverage prospects.

 ➢ Live or deferred telecast.

 ➢ An avenue for expression of the personification of the brand image.

 ➢ Universal appeal among different sections of society.

Music has always had worldwide appeal among different sections of society. Depending on the kind of music of the band/ performer, sponsoring events with which their target audience identifies most. For example, Thumps Up against Pepsi, Coca-Cola - which acquired the brand from Parle - is fighting Pepsi on two fronts. Coke sponsors foreign performers like Whigfield in India and Thumps Up sponsors local performers and bands.

The introduction of satellite channels has given a boost to musical events in that these events provide excellent coverage prospects and a chance for unmatched and exclusive rights to television software for post-event mileage. A live telecast, if possible, gives a great boost to the event and becomes an acclaimed programme for a long time.

Cigarette and liquor firms to consolidate the image of their brands also use stage performances and musical events widely. For example, the Vazir Sultan Tobacco Company sponsors 'Spirit of Freedom' concerts every year providing an opportunity to express the characterisation of the brand image of Charms. Similarly, liquor companies have in the recent past sponsored musical performances such as Ila Arun Live, which had a wild and raunchy air at the show. Musical events also attract multiple sponsors and clients. Generally, one main and a set of co-sponsors are taken on and authorised to utilise the branding opportunities. The venue is generally covered with banners and posters or colours of its sponsors.

C. Cultural Celebrations

Core Concept: Cultural celebrations are get-togethers and celebrations of events that carry mythological, religious importance or have traditional values attached by a specific community with identical features.

Types of celebrations: Fairs and festivals are renowned events in this category. Starting from the countless rural festivals that might also involve business transactions between merchants from far and near to college festivals is basically a get-together. College festivals involve friendly contests and performance by and for the student community, rural fairs and festivals are basically local affairs. Such events include host of smaller events that could be from the other divisions. Fairs and festivals have their foundation in religious tradition and rituals. These were essentially designed to pass on knowledge to the next generation by the elders. For example, the concept of *Holi* evolved from the celebration of a good harvest into a colourful festival heralding spring with an added mythological importance of Vishnu Bhakta Pralhad and his devotion making Holi a festival that combines faith in god as well as celebration of good harvest.

Characteristics: Given the openness, free entry and informality in most of these events, sponsors with innovative interaction points are actually appreciated by the audience. As most of the audience at such events generally walks in on their free will, they are more open. The intervals in between the smaller events also provide interaction opportunities. Since cultural events give greater opportunity for interaction and reach, they provide participating sponsors:

- ➢ A strategy for focusing on a particular community.
- ➢ Reach into the heart of the rural population.
- ➢ A platform for mass communication.
- ➢ An opportunity to communicate to the point.
- ➢ Avoid any sort of clutter.
- ➢ Chance to innovate.
- ➢ Direct sales opportunity.

It is quite an old phenomenon that merchants have been coming to the big fairs and festivals and joining in the celebrations with the common public. Discount offers during the eve of festivals are now a common occurrence.

Another factor connected to the bigger fairs and festivals of India is the rural nature of the events. Rural fairs and festivals are opening up new marketing horizons for the corporate sector. The business sense in sponsoring such an event shows from the fact that television covers barely 18 percent of rural India. Marketers are always on the lookout for ways by which to reach this huge consumer base successfully. Some easy statistics on the fifty largest rural fairs will emphasise the significance of events in the rural context and why they are such an attractive means for sponsors who are pouring out to put their budgets for these festivals.

Table 2.1 is a summary of the number of festivals region-wise which shows that just the top fifty fairs and festivals in India draw a combined audience of almost 5.66 crores. And India has an estimated 5000 different festivals, so imagine the crowd that these would attract. If this event category is ignored, it is not possible to reach the rural population spread over 75,000 villages economically through any other way. Also, these melas not only provide a good audience for communication, they also give companies a unique opportunity of direct selling, free sampling and collection of market research data. Through well-designed campaigns at such fairs it is possible to generate high awareness among the rural population. A fair or festival offers a good platform for mass promotion. The audience on such events is a media buyer's dream.

Table 2.1: Summary of Region-wise Festivals in India.

State	No. of major festivals	Approx. audience in Lakhs
Kerala	19	66
Uttar Pradesh	8	422
Andhra Pradesh	8	17
Tamil Nadu	3	16
Bihar, MP, Haryana	2 each	28
Rajasthan, Gujarat, J&K, HP, Maharashtra, Karnataka	1 each	17
Total	**50**	**566**

With a least amount of spill-over, companies can make a pinpoint communication with a captive audience because these fairs are the only mode of them and plus an added advantage here is that people cannot change channels. In Indian tradition, there are many large scale events whose performances are systematic, that is, these events involve complete sensory awareness, a high level of audience participation and the combination of many art forms like music, dance, poetry as well as people of different faith.

These events provide an opportunity for moving beyond straight sponsorship or visual advertising by permitting innovative methods of promotions to evolve. For example, Colgate splashed its name on Kites during the kite festival in Ahmedabad, Manikchand and Co. had its name 'Oxyrich' almost everywhere in Pune city during Ganesh festival, HLL used a giant boat for a large-sized Life-buoy hoarding at Alwaye in the annual boat race during the Onam festival in Kerala, and so on. Such creative promotions are possible and they guarantee that nobody in the audience misses out on the exposure.

The inter-college festivals, the get-togethers in a student community organised informally by amateurs who come together and work voluntary as co-ordinators and the staff falls completely within the purview of the cultural celebration category. Fergusson, Pune has Oorja, Muktachhanda, St. Xaviers, Bombay has Malhar, IIT, Bombay hosts Mood Indigo. Their web presence and the smooth transition to the 'dot com companies' for sponsorship is very remarkable. To carry out the complete concept is a beautiful work of art in action.

D. Special Business Events

Core concept: Being different and getting noticed for direct commercial gains.

Characteristics: Special business events generally give equal opportunity for reach and interaction. In fact, as these are client driven, most special events are generally interaction-oriented as much as reach-oriented. The whole event is personalised to accommodate the requirement of the clients.

Product Launches: With the entry of multinational brands into India, there has been an unexpected spurt in mega-launch activities using new ideas. The advantage from such events is that the invited audience gets a direct experience of the product. Furthermore, the accompanying media coverage lends much credibility to the product. Creating and celebrating an event is a kind of investment in brand building. In fact, reports say that after a mega-launch using pop music and dance evening as the launch event, Smirnoff was selling two and half times more than it expected to sell in Mumbai. Mega-launches give a flying start to a brand, though how long and how much it would fly depends on the inherent strength of the brand and not on the launch event alone.

Simultaneously, the scale and scope of a launch also depends on the product and its features. A Hutchison Max - GSM provider launched itself in Mumbai in 1999 with a special event. Some firms like an Internet product and IT hardware firms used the Exhibition in 1999 to introduce an exciting range of products and peripherals. This was in tune with the requirement of a target market. Extreme high interaction is needed for a product launch during an exhibition.

E. Retail Events

There is also a growing emphasis being placed on special events by retailers. They all have a general goal – to generate sales. Special events are expected to catch the attention of customer traffic. Thus, customers can be exposed to the products the store wants to sell. Due to the growing importance of special events, some retailers have combined the responsibility for special events with publicity.

Different types of special events are as follows:

1. **Merchandising events:** Merchandising works on the basis of encashing the popularity of events and the core individuals and items concerned with them. When a celebrity visits a store for the event then it is called as a merchandising event. This kind of publicity is done to attract more customers to the store that sells the special items of the event such as T-shirts, teddy bears, dolls, bracelets, caps or any article that becomes famous due to the event. Such merchandising events add to the revenue that an event organiser can earn during and after the actual event.

2. **Demonstrations and showings:** An event which has a low reach and direct interaction, demonstrations are very helpful as part of any event campaign for customers who need to explain the functioning and advantages of their products in detail. Demonstrations such as those given on usage of wigs, kitchen peelers, the V slicer etc. are examples of these. In fact, tele-shopping firms, like TSN, TVC, Teleshopping, Homeshop etc. have organised moving vans carrying the new items shown on television so that people can touch and feel them before buying.

3. **Special sales inducements:** Reach and interaction that a client desires from an event ultimately needs to be changed into tangible purchases by the target audience. Special sales inducement events are right at the cutting edge of this requirement. Two-for-one sales, one-rupee sales, contests and competitions such as slogan writing plus giveaways such as free samples of merchandise, shopping bags, reusable packaging etc. fall under this kind of special events. Just lately, a major branded jeans showroom in downtown Mumbai had offered buyers of goods above a particular amount extra jeans for just ₹1 with resounding success. The offer of buy two Cielos and get one free by Daewoo Motors in mid 1998 is yet another example of special sales inducement events.

4. **Film and Television based events:** Taking advantage of the craze for films, both Hindi and English, firms are adopting different techniques to use this for their benefit. With the introduction of satellite television and proliferation of channels, the audience has got so fragmented that sponsoring the screening of a famous movie is a better option for addressing an audience that is largely drawn from the target section of the company's product. By changing the get-together of stars – from the launch of the shooting of the film that is, Mahurat to the promotion of the film after launch and the celebration of completing different landmark days for the film – into important special events the sponsoring company can get good mileage.

   Though sponsoring film-based events can be very effectual as a promotional tool, it lends a very poor recall rate for the sponsors of most events. A survey conducted put the recall rate for sponsors at 9 percent for a sponsored premiere of a hit Hindi film 'Om Shanti Om' as compared to a high of 43 percent for the sponsors of Miss India from Femina. Features of film based events have the highest reach with least communication. Simultaneously, events mainly designed for the television medium such as Bournvita Quiz contest, Colgate Gel Boogie Woogie, Close-up Antakshari leverage on precisely this prime branding opportunity for their sponsors.

5. **Web-based events:** Just ten years back the idea of using the computer for anything beyond just scientific programming was absent. Today we have web-based seminars, conferences and web-casting that is, broadcasting on the web of events and live transmission of scoreboards of competitive events through the Internet. CricInfo.com was one of the leading sites to launch a live scoreboard for cricket on-line targeting the millions of Indian Cricket enthusiasts. These web-based events and Internet-friendly event information with details are targeted towards bringing interactivity over the web to the net-savvy target audience.

America OnLine (AOL.com) is very active in arranging exclusive live web events ranging from shows featuring Madonna as a guest, to a live coverage of the Olympics and the Presidential elections campaign events. On these live events, AOL subscribers, which are the target audience here, get to watch questions and answers open up in real time, submit questions to the guest, chat with other audience members, re-examine the agenda of upcoming chats and events plus read transcripts of thousands of previous chats and events.

2.2 CLIENTS

The concept of clients for an event organiser comprises a broad spectrum of entities. These entities range from individuals to corporate clients. It is essential that the event organiser focus on particular clients, at least in the initial stages, which they would like to provide their services to.

Clients are the people or companies who act as sponsors at any event. They provide sponsorship for the events because they use events as an effective marketing communication tool to place themselves in the minds of the target market.

They provide funds that either completely or partly give financial assistance to an event so as to make it reasonable for the target audience. The risk rating of an event increases if sufficient funds from sponsors do not support the event, finally affecting the event organisers.

Corporate clients should be educated about the uses and importance of events as a strategic marketing communications tool. The one factor that event savvy firms always pay attention for is greater value addition from the event organisers.

Clients also have to actively involve themselves with the event activities, for extracting higher value from the event. Right from the briefing to the actual implementation of the event, clients also need to be on their toes.

The uses and benefits that one single event can provide, need to be exploited to the maximum. Regardless of how good the event organiser is, the client must be prepared and do their part in the event efficiently. Following steps should be taken by the client in order to perform their part in event management.

1. Set objectives for the event

2. Negotiating contracts with event organisers

3. Locating interaction points, banners, displays etc. at the event

4. Preparing the company's staff for the event

5. Post-event follow-up

2.2.1 Set Objectives For The Event

It is important to set specific objectives for any event. As an event manager, set out your objectives for the event early on by asking yourself why you are running it in the first place. Key questions you should be able to answer are:

➢ What do you want from the event?

➢ What do you want the event to say?

➢ Is the event primarily about giving information? And if so, can you achieve the same objective by sending out a publication or by referring potential delegates to a website instead?

➢ Is the event primarily about the new ideas that can emerge from the interaction? (If so, the sessions will need to be highly participative.)

➢ Who do you want to speak to (that is, who is your audience?)

➢ What do you want your audience to do at the event?

➢ What do you want your audience to do after the event?

Before planning any event, it is important to clearly understand why one is having the event. Be sure to have a thoughtful response for 'why are we holding this event?' This will help to stay focused on the task and motivate to see the objective fulfilled. Key points to keep in mind as one proceeds:

• Have clearly identified objectives for holding the event.

• Set objectives that are SMART: specific, measurable, achievable, realistic and timely.

• Objectives may vary, based on the nature of the event.

Answer the question "Why Events?" as rigorously as possible. Events are a media wherein anything is possible. The greater the depth of thought in terms of the objectives set for the event at this stage, the better the benefits that can be reaped. The benefits desired, need to be communicated clearly to the event organiser. It is important, since the event organiser is entirely dependent on the briefing from the client to create and customise the event concept. Companies often use events through either co-sponsoring an event or customising it for specific objectives. Most often reasons for using a particular event have been made based on excuses such as presence of competitors, inexpensive or cheap availability of the event, or even because the event was used in the previous years. In fact, sometimes companies sponsor events due to the fear that their absence will create negative publicity. Event organisers often exploit such fears.

2.2.2   Negotiating Contracts with Event Organisers

Event organisers are responsible for the production of events from conception through to completion. Events can include exhibitions and fairs, festivals, conferences, promotions and product launches, fundraising and social events. Event organisers work in the public, private and not-for-profit sectors and can work for event management companies, in-house for an organisation or freelance.

Checking on the background of the organisers and their experience in the area is essential. Negotiation with event organisers is also essential. This is so because a company that takes active interest in the event and is in a position to provide a host of support services can cut down the overall cost of the event as well as reduce the direct expenditure on the event. A long-term relationship or promise of participation in other events in the event calendar of the organiser should also show future benefits in terms of assured presence in the event and the reduced cost.

One must also get to know the other sponsors who are being tapped by them for the event and break them down into interested, provisional and confirmed levels. Check on the planned promotional campaign and their strategy to attract the target audience. Does the planned medium entice specify target segments for the companies' products? The number of free tickets offered to the clients, as part of the value for money by the event organiser is also a vital indicator of whether they are relying on the company to bring in the audience. Also, checking on important nitty-gritty's such as the organisers' plans for VIPs, the press, parking, complimentary gifts etc. is a vital part of negotiating with event organisers.

2.2.3 Locating Interaction Points, Banners, Displays etc. at the Event

The objectives set for the particular event should indeed determine the position, size and location of the stall or interaction points with the target audience. The banners and other display materials usually have fixed locations and should be clearly visible and readable. Creative and innovative locations should also be scouted for in and around the venue to extract maximum mileage. Some companies prefer to make a big impact at the main entrance, others insist on a corner site so that they can be approached from more than one side. In fact, if there were an opportunity, then approach from all sides would be ideal. Such a location is usually called as an island site. The answer to this issue can be obtained from understanding clearly, how one wants to deal with the people visiting the stand. It will vary at each show, and must be thought out well in advance.

2.2.4   Preparing the Company's Staff for the Event

It is imperative that the participating staffs are trained for the specific event environment, to derive the maximum value for money spent on the event. This training should be more than just a briefing on the event flow and other details such as where to be at any particular time, etc. An event kit provided to the staff would encourage commitment and participation.

The kit should invariably include:

1. The event details, rules and regulations, dress codes as well as scheduled duties and responsibilities.
2. Times and dates of attendance and details of VIP visits and celebrity openings.
3. Visits from top management and press.
4. Boarding and lodging details.
5. Details of other stalls from other sponsoring companies.
6. Product catalogues and samples.
7. Promotions or competitions and roles therein.
8. A briefing on security and safety related issues.

Top Tips for Event Staff Management

1. Holding a pre-event meeting
2. Keeping the staff informed

2.2.5 Post-Event Follow-Up

Evaluation is important because:

1. You can establish whether you have met your objectives for the event.

2. You can get feedback from your audience on their opinions of how the event was organised and whether their needs were met. This will help you to decide how to take forward your future programme.

3. It can help to identify areas where improvements can be made for future events.

4. Consider supplying participants with an evaluation form. The event organiser should remind people to fill out their form before closing at the end of the day and staff should be on hand to pick up the forms on the delegates' way out. Alternatively, a clearly signed box for the return of the forms should be made available from exit points.

5. Evaluation forms should be collated within a week of the event and general details outlining how the event was should be supplied to them along with a personalised thank you letter.

What you are planning to do post-event should be built in to your planning from the very outset. To wrap up an event, a number of things need to happen.

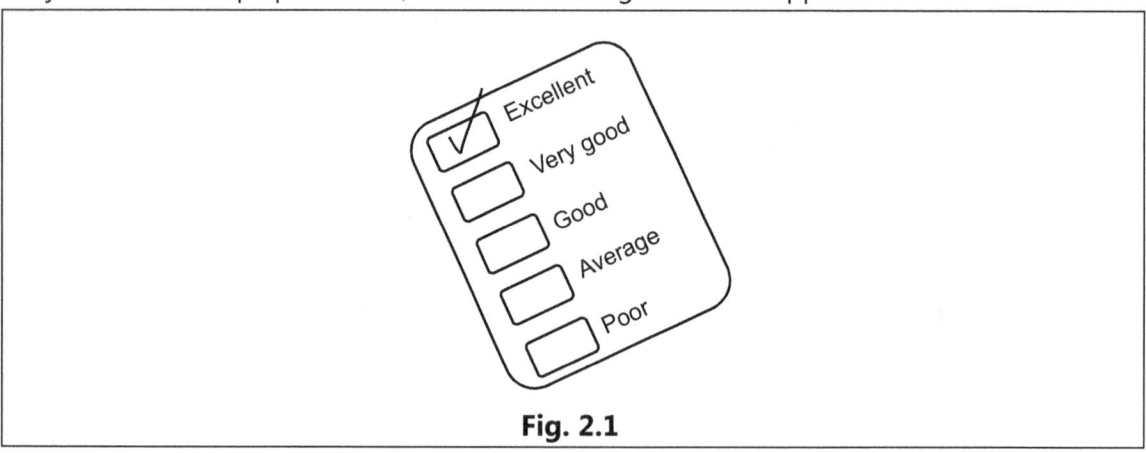

Fig. 2.1

For example, a post-event follow-up after a conference can include:

*   Collating all the feedback forms to assess the success of the event against the original objectives.

*   Deciding whether any further follow-up work is required.

*   Sending letters to all speakers thanking them for their presentation and giving them feedback from the evaluation forms.

- Sending a letter to the chair thanking them for their time and giving them feedback on the day.

- Sending out a press release and photograph to key journalists who expressed an interest in the event but were unable to turn up.

- Providing them with contact details for key speakers so that they can write a post-conference news story or commission a feature based on one of the speaker's presentations.

- Consider publishing a timely post-conference report, including transcripts or summaries of the key speakers' presentations. The report could be sent directly to delegates and made available in PDF format from the website (with an email sent to all delegates and others who were unable to attend). This shouldn't be left too long after the event.

- Deciding if any further actions are required to meet your objectives.

The assumption that after the event, the responsibilities of the company staff are over, is not true. Once the event is over, it should be evaluated as to understand the extent to which the objectives set were achieved and the intended benefits were derived. In fact, the entire idea of the event has to be sustained and maximum benefits, milked from the inquiries and feedback received from the interaction with the customers at the event. In addition, a lesson should be drawn so as to formulate a strategy to derive higher benefits next time if any event is sponsored.

Event Planning Questionnaire

Whether an event planner is a novice or a professional planner, the following questionnaire is useful in identifying elements of the planning process.

Why?

➢   is the event being held

What?

➢   type of event will this be

➢   is the agenda

➢   will be served

➢   will the entertainment be

➢   Equipment is required (audiovisual, microphone, podiums, banners, etc.)

➢   costs are there

When?

➢ is the event

➢ are the planning meetings

➢ are the pre/post parties

➢ should things be set up

➢ should staff/volunteers be there

Where?

➢ will the event be

➢ will the head table and podium be

➢ will people sit (is there a seating plan/are place cards needed)

➢ will the entertainment play

➢ will people park their vehicles

How?

➢ many people are invited

➢ many people will likely to attend

➢ can we get the addresses of the invited guests

➢ will the event be promoted

Who?

➢ will be invited

➢ will co-ordinate the function

➢ will order and plan the decorations

➢ will clean up (pre/post event)

➢ will greet or register guests

➢ will do the coat check

➢ will sell tickets

➢ will be in-charge of the menu

➢ will be a sponsor

2.3   EVENT ORGANISERS

Event organising is a business proposal as any other. Event organisers could be a division of an advertising agency/media house or a professional event organising firm or a group of people within the company given the responsibility for conducting the event. For professional event organisers, event management and event marketing carry different implications though most individuals in the events business call their firms as event management firms. There is a clear line of differentiation between event management and event marketing.

Any event needs a team. How an event organising team is formed and how the responsibilities are shared rely mostly on two factors – the business definition or focus of the events firm regarding the important elements and the definition of clients and target audience. This team may include people who are employees or family members or even freelancers. The team has to be completely involved with every part of the event. Just like advertising agencies, event organisers are now coming into their own.

With the introduction of professional event organisers and the corporatisation of events industry, a new breed of communication professional that of the event professional has taken root in the industry. The need for event organisers is increasing gradually mostly due to four reasons which are as follows

1. The events business needs physical presence of different professionals and running around is a daily affair in this field. The customers' employees may not like such activities.

2. Handling legal hassles such as permissions to be taken from government agencies needs a lot of patience and hard work.

3. Networking with media, facility providers and suppliers is energy sapping work to say the least. This requires complete involvement from the organisers and time may be best for the customers to invest in such activities.

4. The huge amount of experience and expertise in organising particular events, that the clients may never have, also weighs heavily in support of professional event organisers.

Event organisers play a very significant role in brand promotion, new product launches, managing corporate events, award function, fashion shows, etc.

2.3.1 Targeting Clients & Selecting Event Categories to Serve

The concept of clients for an event organiser includes a wide range of entities. These entities range from people to corporate clients. It is important that the event organiser concentrate on specific clients, at least in the beginning, which they would like to provide their services to.

Each event category differs in the effort involved in organising and simultaneously they also vary in their lucrativeness. Due to the different features of each event category, choosing a right portfolio of event categories is a must. It would help in developing the required skill and creating a unique position in the minds of the future clients. Once set, it would be possible to expand into other event categories.

2.3.2 Selecting and Contracting with Other Key Elements in Chosen Categories

Just as targeting the right clients and selecting the specific event categories to serve is significant, it is equally significant that the right mix of other key elements is not only determined, but also contracted for availability and fixation of the rates beforehand. Every event organiser must seriously concentrate on talent management as it is the artist, the sportsperson, the participant or the performer who gives a face to the event and outlines the core around which the concept revolves. It is thus important that the event organiser should build long term relations with the other important elements. A definiteness and purposefulness comes to the planning of the events once the whole portfolio including the important elements is planned out.

2.3.3 Role of an Event Organiser

Event organisers are in-charge of all parts of an event. They play a very crucial role. They co-ordinate all aspects, from the beginning right through to the end, overseeing all the details and ensuring everything gets completed on time and on budget. An event organiser can't start to run an event, without getting all of the groundwork set. It is hands-on and often involves working as part of a team. The role of event organiser varies depending on the organisation and type of event involved. We can enlist those as follows:

1. Researching markets to identify opportunities for events;
2. Liaisoning with clients to determine their precise event requirements;
3. Producing comprehensive proposals for events (for example, timeliness, venues, suppliers, legal obligations, staffing and budgets);
4. Agreeing to and managing a budget;
5. Securing and booking an appropriate location;
6. Guaranteeing insurance, legal, health and safety obligations are followed;
7. Co-ordinating venue management, caterers, stand designers, contractors and equipment hire;

8. Scheduling that is, creating a programme plan of workshops, demonstrations or entertainment for the event;

9. Organising, that is, getting all the right people together at the right time and taking general responsibility for what needs to be done;

10. Organising facilities for car parking, traffic control, security, first aid, hospitality and the media;

11. Identifying and securing speakers or special guests;

12. Planning room layouts and the entertainment programme, scheduling workshops and demonstrations;

13. Co-ordinating staffing requirements and staff briefings;

14. Selling sponsorship/stand or an exhibition space to the potential exhibitors/partners;

15. Preparing delegate packs and papers;

16. Liaising with marketing and PR colleagues to promote the event;

17. Liaising with clients and designers to form a brand for the event and organising the production of tickets, posters, catalogues and sales brochures;

18. Liaising that is, keeping everyone involved with the event informed and up-to-date with all the latest developments. This comprises everyone from the clients and the marketers promoting the event right through the designers making the tickets for the events;

19. Co-ordinating suppliers, handling client queries and troubleshooting on the day of the event to guarantee that all runs smoothly;

20. Tidying up and taking stock at the end;

21. Supervising the dismantling and elimination of the event and clearing the venue efficiently;

22. Post-event assessment (including data entry and analysis and generating reports for event stakeholders).

23. Looking back over the event and seeing what went well and what can be improved.

2.3.4 Qualities of an Event Planner/Organiser

Admittedly, it takes a very specific type of person to become an event planner or organiser. It is an industry where one's experience matters less than his ability to think things through logically and solve problems quickly, on your feet. There are certain, inherent qualities, personality traits and professional aptitudes that just can't be taught, but which are essential to become a great event planner or organiser. Job description of a standard event planner/ organiser might not list out the actual qualities; it is something that is implied with the position.

Here are some important skills or qualities, an event planner/organiser should have.

1.   An understanding of logistics. This is and has always been an important skill for an organiser. Our organiser has to know about room layouts, the tendency of people when queuing and where the best stands will probably be located on a floor-plan. They also are required to consider sight lines, maximum room capacities and a thousand other things that no longer easily fall under the jurisdiction of 'operations.'

2.   Marketing. No one has the event so close to their heart as the event organiser. This is why knowing the discipline of marketing an event is a must have skill. One should have marketing skills to motivate guest to attend conferences, or be well-informed about product launches or business grand openings.

3. 'Experience' not event design. In order to guarantee that the events are more than 'people and logistics' a deep knowledge of meeting design is important for the reborn 'Event Organiser'. It's not just the learning environment that has to be thought about but an understanding of the psychology of attendees which even filters down to their on-site food and beverage consumption.

4. Social Media. Understanding the role of Social Media in promoting and involving attendees in the events is a new but undeniably and important weapon in the 'rounded organisers' arsenal.

5. Event Technology. With mobile apps, voting and engagement pads, gamification and all manner of gadgets and gizmos, our organiser has to be 'tech' savvy like never before. This is why an event like Tech Fest exists.

6. Hybrid Events. The extent of hybrid events has yet to be measured correctly but there is no doubt that it will be a bigger player in the world of events. Together with its sisters 'live streaming' and 'web casting' our organiser has to have complete information on new ways of delivering the content and experiences.

7. Budgetary control. Instead of keeping to a rigid set budget the organiser has to design this budget to guarantee that value is added to all of the parties involved in the event while bringing in the target profit.

8. Negotiation. It is a very conventional function and still a core skill for the organiser. But even this has changed: it's not now just about getting the lowest price. Organisers must control Social Media, other forms of marketing and think about how to give an experience of the event to the suppliers. This approach concentrates on adding value as well as functioning for the right fees and charges for locations, speakers and even other suppliers.

9. A people person. It is that part of the role that has and will never change, determined but approachable, decisive but flexible, Fun but serious. On site and in planning this aspect of the role is an essential part to an events success.

10. A true industry representative. These modern day organiser has to be more like 'Mighty Mouse' than a 'Teddy Bear'. The multitalented organiser has to represent an industry still struggling to be recognised and appreciated. One has to be active and has to tell the importance of events to several kinds of companies in several different sectors.

In addition to these, event planners/organisers must have excellent communication skills, he should be able to liaise with others and do basic administration, he should be enthusiastic and be well organised. In brief, he should be able to juggle multiple responsibilities.

...............[Before the event, have person/committee -in-charge of:

- Sponsors
- Local Participants
- Chief Guest, Speakers,
- Designing, Printing, Collection of Articles and evaluation of the same
- Prizes, Mementos, Gifts, Banners, Certificates, Souvenirs
- Transportation, Caterers, Venue Arrangement, Decorations, Backdrop, Parking
- Media, PR, Marketing]...............

On the day of event have person(s) in charge of:

- Overall Coordination
- Green Room
- Food
- On Stage Activities
- Master of Ceremony
- Computer, LCD projector,
- Photographer
- Reception

- Crowd Management and PR with Crowd
- Parking Area
- Security

Distribution of Various things (Gifts, Certificates to selected people as well as all the Participants)

2.3.5 Steps in Organising an Event

When you are organising an event, then you need to ponder on following points.

1. Idea and Concept

Once you have an idea about how to plan an event, remember to be flexible. Give yourself some space for changing and developing the idea. Once you settle on some idea, move on to developing the concept of the event. The concept will give you more competitive advantage; it is what will make your event stand out from events that are similar. The event concept can consist of things like design, collaboration and partnerships with firms, technology, location, and others. These days, most event planners aim to hold eco-friendly events, which consists of recycling, focusing on online advertisement and others. Remember, you are not just holding an event; you are creating an experience for your audience.

2. Determine the audience

Determining the audience for your event should never be taken lightly. Your audience is the key to find the right sponsors and partners. So, ask yourself these questions: Is my event different, and will specific types of individuals/businesses show up? Previously, what audience have the event speakers I have in mind, attracted? Considering the price of attendance, what groups will attend? If it's too costly, maybe students will not be eager to attend. Be prepared to give discounts and establish a promotion time. Also, consider the place and time of the event to estimate who can attend.

3. Create the agenda

Once you have finalised your concept and estimated the expected audience, start thinking about the event's schedule. Do you want to have a whole day event; is it going to be a workshop, going for a few weeks? Who are the speakers you can invite? Depending on your answers, you can start searching the right venue, partners and sponsors.

4. Find the right venue

The venue is very important. For an all-day conference, a congress centre is suitable; on the other hand, you're having workshops, a place where there is close group effort of attendees. In any case, prepare a proposal of partnership for your chosen site. The objective is to find a venue with which you have common interests so that you can negotiate well.

5. Invite speakers

In order to draw speakers to your event, you should have a well-developed event plan that shows passion and inspiration, so that you can offer them a list of irresistible benefits following their attendance. For each speaker these will be different, but a common one is popularisation of their name/brand among a targeted audience, plus an advertising opportunity. Don't be sad if someone declines to take part, rather be prepared to change your proposal and always have a few other lecturers in mind.

6. Find partners

Partnerships are not as difficult to get as it may sound. Contact coffee and water suppliers, so that you provide some drinks at your event. You can also offer design students to expand their portfolio by creating promotional and other materials for the event.

7. Find sponsors

Firstly, you need to think carefully which firms and organisations will be interested in sponsoring your event and what are the benefits this sponsorship offers them. Sponsoring firms are interested in the event's audience and topic when they decide whether or not your event is a suitable place to promote their brand. Sponsorship is also a way of connecting brands.

8. Find Marketing and Media Partners

You need to think whether it is possible to have a sufficient marketing campaign. There are some ways to get around pricey on and offline advertising. Firstly, there is social media, which you can handle yourself with a bit of interest. You can find a lot of information online on how to use social media for promotion and the kind of mistakes you should steer clear of at all costs. Yet, one of the most powerful tools for online promotion is to have persuasive content to share with your audience. Finding media partners to discuss your event, showcasing interviews and reviews on TV would be a great beginning for your marketing campaign. The media will give you authority, so ensure that you find at least one respected media partner.

9. Find website

Website design can really drain half of your budget, so instead, try to do it yourself. Many solutions like Word press and Wix offer great services for creating a customised website for free. You won't need any extensive HTML knowledge and you will avoid hosting costs.

10. Choose your event management software wisely

Consider 2 things

o   Avoid working with services asking for upfront payments.

o   Avoid working with services holding back your money.

Before selecting your event management and ticketing software look thoroughly for a solution that will actually work *for* you. Consider the choices you are offered and the corresponding pricing. You should choose the solution that gives you the most flexibility and customisation options without tying you to third parties. Also, it is wise to research on the software's fee collection process; otherwise you might end up negatively surprised by your money being withdrawn because of transaction procedures.

11. Build your pricing carefully

The pricing plan of your event has an important role in the decision-making process of many attendees. Try to estimate your budget correctly. Once again, be prepared to establish promotional times and discounts.

12. Go live

Going live is the final step before the event itself. Once your event goes live, be prepared to answer the question and check your results every hour so that you can adjust your plans according to the situation.

2.4   VENUE

A venue is the site at a desired location with the required audience capacity and available for a particular time period where the event concept shall be performed. Venues are generally created not for core concepts but for a particular variation of a core concept. The best example that can be presented is in the sporting arena. Separate stadiums are built for cricket, hockey, football, basketball etc. This is a fact found not only in India but also worldwide.

An sport was just an example. Similar customised venues exist for musical concerts (Rang Bhavan in Mumbai), Exhibitions (World Trade Centre, Discovery of India Building in Mumbai) and of course, other event variations such as the many halls for weddings and other religious purposes etc.

Though this is a standard practice, it is completely up to the discretion of the venue management to permit events of other sections to take place at their site. For example, it is again pretty common to find music concerts being arranged at sports venue though there are certain music halls and parks available. This might be because of constraints as a result of availability, the capacity, and rate or infrastructure requirements demanded by the event concept. On the other hand, this is not a completely favourable situation. Events implemented on venues meant for other categories of events entail hardships that are avoidable.

2.4.1 Choosing a Venue

The location and venue are critical to the success of any event. For finding venue, one needs to consider some issues such as:

1. **Size of the Event:** The larger is the event, the fewer are the number of venues that will be able to accommodate it. To get the venue of the choice one needs to plan early. Some of the premier conference venues hosting 200 ++ people get booked up a year in advance although most large hotels offer good conferencing facilities.

Fig. 2.2

2. **Length of the Event:** If one can do the business in just a couple of hours, a breakfast or evening briefing, or a short seminar, may work better. If speakers or delegates are likely to require overnight accommodation (either because they are coming from far or because the event will last longer than a day), one needs to choose a venue that has hotel accommodation close by. Delegates don't like to travel far between the two.

3. **Type of Event:** What atmosphere should be conveyed? If it's informal and for a small group, an evening reception or breakfast briefing with opportunities for networking may

be considered. If it is formal and for a large group, a conference or a seminar may work better. Ideally for a large conference, one main conference room; one room for catering (this should be separate from the main conference room as the caterers will need to set up which can be noisy); one area adjacent to the main room for registration (this could be the same space as the catering area) and breakout rooms should be booked.

4. **Format:** The event organiser needs to decide the layout of the main room. For example, does he wants the people seated around tables (cabaret style), which will halve the number, of accommodation or does he prefers people to be seated in rows (theatre style)? How many breakout rooms for workshops will be required and in what layout should they be? If there is a question and answer session, one may also need to provide a roving mike. Most conferences and events over 30 people also require a podium for speakers and a top table with nameplates.

5. **Location:** The venue should be chosen which is in easy reach of public transport links (particularly train or tube links), making it best to choose one of the main metropolitan areas. However, if the conference is about urban renewal and you want to take delegates on a tour of an area undergoing change, then that will clearly help to influence the location for the conference. In general, the harder it is for delegates to travel to a location, the less likely they will bother to come. Consideration should also be given to whether the speakers or delegates will require overnight accommodation. If so, the venue should be close by.

6. **Facilities offered at the Venue:** Delegates might need to be offered a business desk providing email, fax and a telephone service for urgent enquiries. Other facilities that could be useful include photocopying and message taking.

7. **Accessibility:** Any venue one chooses should be fully accessible to people with disabilities. As well as offering lifts and ramps for wheelchair users, a hearing loop should be provided for delegates with a hearing impairment.

The most important factor when considering a venue is the availability factor. The amount of time that the venue is required for the event is a summation of the actual event time and the time required for completion of the pre and post event activities, that is, erection and dismantling of the infrastructure involved.

The capacity of the venue is another major issue. The demands of the event concept decided from the brief have to be met. Since the rates for the venue also form a major portion in the costing for the event, a venue should be considered only if it meets the requirements as defined by the concept since capacity and infrastructure available have a decisive impact on the rates for the venue. Rates for venues vary with the season for the event. Each category of event or a particular variation may have a certain peak season when the event is very popular and in demand.

...........Factors to be considered while selecting a venue and negotiating the price:

- Capacity of the Hall (No. of Delegates --excluding floating delegates)
- Provision for Food (if meals are served)
- Timing (When does the event can start and end at the venue)
- Lighting arrangement (in case for night events)
- Air-conditioned or not
- Required Equipment are provided (Mikes, Speakers, etc)
- Furniture for dais (Tables, Chairs, Table Clothes)
- Whether Music, Entertainment is allowed or not (for informal programs)
- Power Backup
- Accessibility -- whether the venue is centre of city (Whether Delegates can arrive without any difficulty)
- Special Rooms for Organisers, Dressing up etc
- Total Cost.....................

2.4.2 Types of Venues

There are two types of venues, in-house and external and these should also be kept in mind during the conceptualisation process. Sometimes the concept has to be modified to suit the realities of the venue and this can distort the costing beyond estimation. Therefore, the importance of general guideline should be kept in mind by the event organisers while scouting for a venue. It is also very essential that the suitability of indoor or outdoor venues should be checked out.

Basic infrastructure such as cool drinking water, fan, lighting and hygiene arrangements are a necessity at every venue is meant for. A proper inquiry should be done for the caterers and decorators, which may be prevalent at most venues. Contingencies, such as power failures need to be tackled and the need for generators should be properly assessed. Contingency plans need to be built for disruptions that can be caused due to the changes in weather. The performance area should be designed based on the load that is to be carried within the area available and at such a height that it is clearly visible to the maximum number of people. Most venues have standard restrictions. These restrictions should be understood clearly since these could be decor, food and beverages, monopolies, working hours, holidays or smoking restrictions. The mode and type of payments for venues depend on the arrangement that is negotiated.

Though these guidelines may not be comprehensive, it covers the entire spectrum of operational points to be kept in mind while making a decision on selection of a venue.

2.4.3 In-house Venue

Any event that is executed within the premises of the firm or institution or in the private homes or properties belonging to the client is called an event at an in-house venue. Big companies generally have conference rooms, halls or open spaces within their firms and their campuses where events can be held.

The advantage of such arrangement is the huge saving in the costs incurred in hiring the venue. The use of such facilities is reserved for the employees of the firm or residents of the campus.

An indoor venue entails the necessity to check on the availability of air conditioning. The maximum seating capacity is worked out based on the area and may increase or decrease for different events and venues depend on the performance area and visibility of this area to the audience. The quality of the facilities such as interiors, acoustics, ambience, cleanliness and other technical requirements should be meticulously defined and provided for.

(a): In-house Venue

(b): In-house Venue

Fig. 2.3

2.4.5 External Venue

Any venue, over which neither the client nor the professional event organisers have any ownership rights, is external venue. These venues can be rented by anyone and is open for the general public. Generally hotels have halls and rooms particularly meant for particular events that can be utilised either by corporate, individuals, families etc. Most events are held at external venues.

Fig. 2.4

Some events are actually venue-driven. Small budget events and theme parties for celebration of festivals or some special days see the venues playing the clients' role for the event organisers, for example, amusement parks.

Points to Remember

- Event infrastructure includes the essential elements - core concepts, core people, core talent, and core structure, without which there cannot be any event.

- As an Event Manager, set out your objectives for the event by asking yourself the key question "Why Events?" as rigorously as possible. Events are a media wherein anything is possible.

- Negotiation with event organisers is also essential because a company that takes active interest in the event and is in a position to provide a host of support services can cut down the overall cost of the event as well as reduce the direct expenditure on the event.

- Position, size and location of the stall or interaction points with the target audience should really be determined so as to be approachable from more than one side.

- The banners and other display materials usually have fixed locations and should be clearly visible and readable.

- It is important to prepare the company's staff for the specific event environment to derive the maximum value for money spent on the event.

- The event needs to be evaluated. Collate all the feedback forms to assess the success of the event against the original objectives.

- Evaluation helps to identify areas where improvements can be made for future events to understand the extent to which the objectives set were achieved and the intended benefits were derived.

- Event organisers are given the responsibility for carrying out the event.

- Event organisers play a very important role in brand promotion, new product launches, managing corporate events, award function, fashion shows, etc.

- The concept of clients for an event organiser comprises of a broad spectrum of entities. These entities range from individuals to corporate clients.

- Selecting a right portfolio of event categories is a must. It would help in developing the required expertise and creating a unique position in the minds of the prospective clients.

- A definiteness and purposefulness comes to the planning of the events once the entire portfolio comprising of the key elements is planned out.

- A venue is the site at a desired location with the required audience capacity and available for a specific time period where the event concept shall be carried out.

- While choosing a venue, event organiser should consider the issues like Length of the event, Size of the event, Type of event, Format, Location, and Facilities offered at the venue, Accessibility.

- There are two types of venues, in-house and external.

- Any event that is executed within the premises of the company or institution or in the private homes or properties belonging to the client is called an event at an in-house venue.

- Any venue, over which neither the client nor the professional event organisers have any ownership rights, is external venue.

Questions for Discussion

1. What do you mean by event infrastructure? Explain its essential elements?

2. Explain the importance/necessity/significance of setting objectives of the event.

3. What do you understand by target audience?

4. What is post-event follow-up? Explain the importance of evaluation.

5. Explain the role of event organisers. Why is the need for event organisers increasing day by day?

6. What are the key elements to be stressed by event organisers while planning for the event?

7. What are the criteria for the selection of a venue? Explain in-house venues and external venues.

Chapter 3...

Execution of Event

Contents ...

Learning Objectives ...

After going through this chapter, you will be able to gain an insight into the following

- To study the networking components for the promotion of events.
- To understand and get acquainted with the activities in event management.
- To study types of promotion methods used in event management.
- To get acquainted with the concept of EMIS that is, Event Management Information System.
- To understand the role and importance of technology in event management.

3.1 NETWORKING COMPONENTS

Promotion in events is required to get the desired reach that requires an adequately planned publicity campaign by the event marketer. The event marketer has to network with other media for successful publicity of an event.

There are a number of networking components like print media, radio, television, internet, cable network, and the outdoor media, which are involved in the process of promotion. In this chapter, we will study the important features of these networking components.

3.1.1 Print Media

Pre-event publicity is done with the help of print media and it also aids in the post-event recall by reporting or covering the event as in reporting the success or failure of an event.

Pre-event print media campaign is very essential since it can be used not only to inform about the exact details of the event such as venue, date and time; but also to distribute entry forms or feedback questionnaires. Giveaways and contests are usually associated with such campaigns. The pre-event publicity, which aids in increasing reach is usually paid for or bartered with the media owners as the media sponsors.

The post-event coverage falls under the purview of journalism and usually the event organiser has little control over it and that's precisely why even a failure can get reported.

What is to be publicised using the print media essentially revolves around the variety of publications available, their circulation, the frequency of publication, whether weekly/daily/morning/evening, and the profile of readers. A decision to use a particular newspaper or magazine or a combination of the same will normally depend on the objective to be achieved from the event. For regular festivals and other most popular events, most newspapers and magazines usually plan special supplements, pages or cutouts. Some examples of event specific issues in the recent past are St. Valentine's Day, Holi, Diwali, the 50th year of India's Independence and III Commonwealth Youth Games 2008 held in Pune. Such event specific issues are good because of two reasons:

➢ Special rates for advertising are charged for insertions in such issues.

➢ The state of readiness of the audience is an added bonus since they are prepared and anticipate such issues. And the fact that they look forward to such issues for more information provides more focused reach for the event.

3.1.2   Radio

For pre-event publicity, the radio is widely and mainly used as an electronic audio media. It also has importance in terms of post-event coverage which is thus planned accordingly. The programme profile, the listening audience profile and time slots for airing the commercials are the major decision making criteria. The need to create a jingle or putting together an appealing audio promotion may be expensive and thus this media needs to be understood better as to how and when it is beneficial to use it.

Special programmes with the event as focus and which are more than just a commercial are more helpful in providing the reach that is desired for the event though they may be expensive. For example, the recently held unique talent hunt contest – 'Talent Ekdum Loaded' held at Oberoi Mall, Goregaon, Mumbai. Though not a full-fledged programme on the event, the script for the host was modified as to thread together an interview with the winner Mr. Abhijeet as part of the fillers during the programme. Live telephone calls congratulating Abhijeet were also aired on the programme.

3.1.3   Television

The television media is the single most potent media for events. This is because it can provide pre-event coverage, during event coverage and post-event coverage. Either satellite channels or the government controlled terrestrial channels can be used, depending on the reach desired. The singularly most important feature that television as a media offers is the ability to cover events live that is, during the event itself. The immense popularity of competitive events and especially sports are derived from this factor. Unlike the print media that comes out with special supplements, satellite television offers dedicated channels for music, sports, news etc. This again provides an opportunity to narrow down the reach to focus on the audience for the particular event category.

Frequency of airing the promotions and their timings are very crucial. An event such as a multi-city (focusing only on the metros) concert tour of a pop music band would not prefer DD1 but prefer to promote and tie-up with an exclusive music channel for all its promotions and event coverage. This provides a focused approach to the event. Slotting the promotions after checking on the TRP rating of programmes and their nature would help in positioning the event to the proper target audience. Music concerts invariably have one of the numerous music channels as an exclusive media sponsor. The Coca-Cola Alisha Chinai Concert Tour, organised by Unirapport events, used the television medium extensively to promote the event. Slick promotions were aired on the 24-hour MTV.

3.1.4   The Internet

The multimedia deals with more than one media at the same time in all the fields. It offers unlimited opportunities as it integrates the print, audio and video media. An Internet site can be anything from a web page to a web site that offers audio and video experience. Developments in technology on the e-commerce front have added an entirely brand new angle to the concept of Internet and how it can be used for leveraging an event.

The internet is now extensively used in events for:

➢   Online registration for events.

➢   Dispensing information – both pre and post-event, in the form of databases.

➢   Carrying out complex analysis of information obtained.

➢   Providing e-commerce related opportunities.

Computer games or simulations that evolve out of an event can be offered on sites to add to the experiences of the target audience who surf the net for the information of the event. Sponsors' advertisements with links to their sites are displayed on the site. An advantage of using Internet sites for reaching out to the target audience is that it allows the recording of the number of hits that is, people visiting the site. Adding to this is the possibility of instantaneous information (as against data) collection as well as instant merchandising through e-commerce helping in impulse buying. For example, the official site of XIX Common Wealth Games, 2010 (www.cwgdelhi2010.org) carried banner ads from its sponsors. The home page of this site carried banner ads of lead partner - Indian Railways (भारतीय रेल) and also identified Central Bank of India as the official banking partner. The other main pages also alternatively carried the banners of logos of all the partners, sponsors and co-sponsors. Green Games and Games village ads also were featured on the main pages in a smaller size. The e-commerce shops on this official web site supported Visa transactions, and were offered an opportunity to shop for CWG goodies, memorabilia and collectibles. For subscribing to the CWG Newsletter by providing their email addresses, surfers were offered a chance to win a free pin.

Fig. 3.1: Logo of the Official Sponsor – Lead Partner the Delhi 2010 Commonwealth Games.

The company Hewlett Packard – the official computer and support system provider for the website and the information systems for the 1998 World Cup Soccer in France back in 1998, and the official host of the domain for the world cup football - provided online coverage as well as history, statistics and a million statistical data on the World Cup matches as well as details on the players and their backgrounds at the fingertips of the web surfer. All official publicity material for the World Cup carried the Internet site address and this site played host to all the other official sponsors and was expected to generate 10-20 million hits per day during the football mania. It was expected to provide accreditation and other facilities to 12,000 staff, players and officials. It was also expected to provide access to 10,000 journalists. The solution required almost 75 different HP products to be used. The age of the mega-events, which can be handled without any hassles, had arrived.

The numerous Internet sites that mushroomed to cover yet another extravaganza – the Cricket World Cup'99 in England is also a testimony to the increasing popularity of the Internet to promote and at the same time reap benefits from events.

3.1.5 Cable Network

Nowadays the cable network is a medium which is growing rapidly in popularity. It is most beneficial for a highly localised reach and coverage of events, growing rapidly in popularity. The live as well as deferred coverage of the local Navratri Dandiya by the various cable networks is one of the most popular shows during the Dandiya season. Similarly, coverage of the processions during Ganeshotsav in Mumbai and Pune and also Durga Puja in Calcutta are also very widely watched. The low rates of advertising on this media are also an involving networking with the cable channels is normally based on the localities that the channel covers and number of cable-connected homes.

There are greater chances of the reach losing its significance, as producing television promotions are a very costly proposition and given that the reach offered is tremendous. For example, for an event to be held locally in a metro with a limited capacity, there is no point in promoting the event on DD1 since these are accessible everywhere in India including the rural parts that is required. Over and above the focused reach the cable networks provide, more sponsor friendly as in letting the sponsor have a greater say in the programming as well as giving more time and more time slots for commercials. A ticker tape like ad-line that runs on the bottom of the television screen is just an example of how cable operators do the balancing act between the sponsor and their customers. The customers do not mind it so long as the service obtained is of a good quality.

3.1.6 Outdoor Media

Outdoor media is very essential for pre-event publicity. These are short time span networking elements located at prominent sites usually earmarked for the same. Prime locations, size and number of hoardings, posters and banners are the main decisions to be taken when planning outdoor media. Hoarding sites need to be rent based on the rates that are again dependent on the site location, dimensions of the hoarding and whether these are lighted or not. Hoardings usually carry only broad event awareness messages and are designed for a relatively larger reach than banners and posters. These are usually few in number and far apart from each other. Best locations for hoardings are places where large masses of people are in transit that is, locations such as along the highways, railway stations and railway lines. The fact that the audience is in transit ensures that the number of people who notice and are aware of the hoarding is large.

Banners also carry general awareness information and may actually be a smaller replica of the hoardings. They are repeated at shorter distances and therefore, more effective in catching the attention of the target audience. Banners are designed and put up in and around the localities or places where the target audience can be found to either reside or gather in good numbers. Posters are usually printed and stuck in areas where the target audience population assembles and carries greater details on the event. An advantage that posters offer is that they are not only easier to put up but also can be stuck or pinned up on notice boards or in other prominent locations where people cannot miss them. Posters are directed at small groups of around 2 to 5 people at a time depending on the dimensions of the poster. Further to these, handouts are also printed and distributed lavishly to the target audience population directly either by hand or by delivering the event pamphlet through the local newspaper vendor directly to the homes or offices of the target audience. This becomes an almost one-to-one campaign. For example, Aptech board exams uses a good number of hoardings, banners and posters around schools all over Mumbai to publicise the same.

3.1.7 Social Media

Social media is fast becoming an indispensable part of an event planner's toolbox. Social media is described as a type of website that is based on user generated content and user participation. Examples of social media sites are Twitter, LinkedIn and Facebook, as well as blogs and forums and sites that have user generated content such as the customer reviews on Amazon.

Event organisers can use social media to aid in the planning of events, promotion of events and the management of the event follow up. Social networking sites such as LinkedIn, Facebook and Twitter are all free to use and are a brilliant way of promoting events and encouraging delegates and potential delegates to engage with each other before an event takes place.

However, social media does not have to be used only during the promotion process alone. Social media sites are great at helping companies to encourage discussion, networking and debates about events during the actual event and long after it has finished.

During an event, the organisers should try and encourage delegates to continue talking about and promoting it through social media channels. Event managers should create a Twitter hashtag exclusively for the event and persuade delegates to update their own Twitter feeds with tweets about the event using this hashtag. This means that every delegate at your event, or anyone interested in your event can immediately see what people are doing and saying about it.

During the event promotion stage, event managers should have created a Facebook page specifically for the event. If there are fans of the Facebook page attending the event, event planners can encourage them to add content, such as photos, videos and links. The more user generated content on the various social media sites, the better.

Once the event is over, it is important to persist with the social media use to ensure communication with delegates is kept high and to give delegates a channel through which they can continue their networking with other delegates.

3.2 TYPES OF PROMOTION METHODS USED IN EVENTS

Event promotion is one of the necessities for getting event in front of the audience. There are numerous ways to promote an event. Some organisers use any one method, while others may use combination of different methods. Regardless of type of event, a strong set of promotional strategies can help in promoting the event in a favourable light with the audience.

3.2.1   Sales Promotions and Audience Interaction

In sales promotion, direct marketing is the media where actual interaction with audience takes place. Schemes built on the foundation of the event are used to link merchandising opportunities with the event build up and popularity. Pre-event response sheets with contests and giveaways as incentives may be used to monitor the reactions and responses that the target audience is generating toward the event. Such exercises help in gathering a fair idea as to the actual attendance that can be anticipated for the event. These also help in identifying changes in the networking mix or messages if required.

3.2.2   Public Relations

Reporting of the event is a purely journalistic activity and supposed to be devoid of any undue influence. It is not like the paid media publicity, which is one hundred percent under the control of the event organisers. Absolutely important both pre and during the event, public relations activities focus on giving a fair treatment to the event. These are also directed towards creating an atmosphere of harmony and avenue for providing information on the event. If a major event is going to be organised, it is unnecessary to say that it will catch the attention of many reporters' at large papers as well as television news channels. Thus, it becomes important that the Public Relation activities be well planned. Press conferences, press relations, invites to events for sponsors are some means of networking for good public relations. Public relation is also significant in the event that controversies start arising before the show starts. Though public relation has traditionally been covered in post-event damage control, pro-active public relation involves recognising and creating rapport with press reporters and networking with influencers in order to maintain a positive image of the event organisers over and above a specific event public relation activity.

3.2.3   Merchandising

Events give a chance for physical manifestation of concepts. Most products are generated from the event and can be considered as a synchronised launch for these particular products by default. Unlike free giveaways, such products actually have a commercial value and can be sold just like any other product.

Event specific merchandising can be used for publicity before, during and after the event. Events based on Sports have conventionally provided opportunities for successfully encashing on the merchandising opportunities that get produced. T-shirts on the basis of the colours of famous teams or carrying pictures of star performers, toys and electronic games based on the event are only a few examples of such opportunities. One such example that can be cited on the successful use of event merchandising is Cavallino group which is a fast growing apparel firm with expertise in online retail sales, trackside and event sales, wholesale distribution and licensed merchandise. Cavallino uses sales booth at major car race events throughout the year to expand partner brands. Such innovative products boost the aura and atmosphere around the event – which is so very significant. Entry passes, T-shirts, publicity brochures and posters show off corporate logos. Round–the-clock announcements, video scopes – where corporates screen their advertisements, and stalls to promote their products – are among the regular pay-offs demanded by corporates in return for their corporate dollar or rupee.

3.2.4 In-venue Publicity

The visibility, size and location of the sponsors' in-venue signage are essential for publicity during the actual event. The exhibit shown below depicts the prime spots that were sold to sponsors of the 2000 NFL league football game between the Oakland Raiders and Seattle Seahawks at the Network Associates Coliseum, Oakland, California – the venue for the match.

Table 3.1: Sponsorship at Venues

Sponsorship at Venues

- ***Northside Electronic Score Board Sponsors with the larger screen.*** The Oakland Tribune (ANG newspapers), UA Local Union #342 (plumbers, steam fitters, refrigerators, Northern MCA California), IKON Office Solutions, 24 Hr Fitness, Web TV, Pepsi, Office Depot (taking care of business).

- ***Southside Electronic Score Board Sponsors*** Web TV, Bud – King of Beer, 24 Hr Fitness, Ford Dealership – Northern California, KICU – TV home of the A. Communications: Avaya Communications, Beverages: Pepsi.

- ***Other Sponsors at the Mid-level Stands*** ValueStar.com, Alhambra, Macy's, Men's wearhouse, Silverdo – Country Club and Resort, Budweiser, Tickets.com, Carsmart.com, McAfee.com.

Sometimes, events shown on the television such as sports, determine the location of the in-venue publicity hoardings of sponsors' banners. As shown in the above Table 3.1, the arrows A, B, C and D show the locations where the TV cameras repeatedly show on the TV screen and cover extensively. These are the two scoreboards, the two bunkers from where the teams surface on the field, stand directly behind the goals and other sites where the TV camera might concentrate on during the game. Therefore, the audience at the game is not exposed to advertisements that are cluttered all over and the TV commercials, during the strategically slotted breaks focused on the audience watching the event live on TV.

There are different kinds of sports such as water sports, motor sports, track and field events that may be either individual or team-based. Each game attracts particular sponsors such as motor sports catch the attention of firms involved with lubricants, oil, tyre etc. This need not be universally appealing to the different individual firms. Honda takes a lot of pride in being connected to motor sport events. In India, MRF and JK Tyres take exceptional interest in such sports. In fact, being connected to go-kart tracks that are still exotic in nature for Indian audiences is also an accorded importance.

Logos, banners, posters and handouts are designed to deliver the promises made for the event. The audience use these handouts and flyers as guides for the show. Special banners are made to draw attention to the contests, invite participation in different activities and sales promotions are different from those used for outdoor promotions.

Unlike outdoor media, which publicise the whole event, in-venue signage, works at a micro level and publicises individual parts of the event plan. For example, say in a college festival like IIT Bombay's Mood Indigo, a major attraction of the whole event is the Aqua Games, a concept invented by Mood Indigo. Aqua Game is a concept where fun lovers play games in the swimming like Chivalry Race, Tug of War, Burma Bridge etc. organised daily with an audience of around 2000, this micro event offers a chance for companies to sponsor for the event as well as get publicity.

In-venue publicity opportunities provided at such an event that concentrates on youth would be printing and distribution of Aqua Games T-shirts, caps and sun shades with the sponsors' logo, locating stall(s) near the pool and inviting people to take part in sales promotion activities such as slogan, writing contests etc. and exhibiting banners at the poolside. Announcement of the sponsor's name by the comparers on timely basis is also a very potent publicity opportunity as the audience is almost hooked on to every word spoken by the comparers. Yet another chance to make an impact during the event and at the venue is to give gift hampers as prizes for the games at event. This generally leaves a lasting impression on the audience at the venue.

3.2.5 Direct Marketing

The term "direct marketing" is originated by Lester Wunderman, considered to be the father of contemporary direct marketing. Direct marketing is practiced by businesses of all sizes, from the smallest start-up to the leaders on the Fortune 500. Direct marketing occurs when businesses address customers through a multitude of channels, including mail, e-mail, phone, and in person. Direct marketing messages involve a specific "call to action," such as "Call this toll-free-number" or "Click this link to subscribe." The results of such campaigns are immediately trackable and measurable, as a business can track responses, results and cost from prospects and/or customers, regardless of medium.

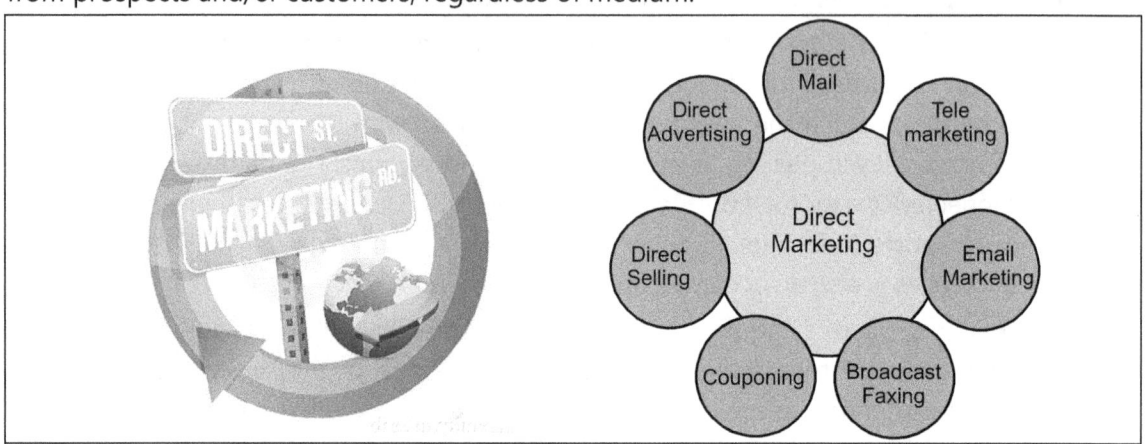

Fig. 3.2

Direct marketing is attractive to many marketers because its positive results can be measured directly. Measurement of results is a fundamental element in successful direct marketing.

Success of any Direct Marketing campaign, in terms of number of times the desired response may vary between the best vs. the worst of the following parameters, depends on:

- List or targeting
- Offer
- Timing
- Ease of response
- Creativity
- Media employed. The medium/media used to deliver a message can have a significant impact on responses.

In sum, choosing the best of all the above parameters may yield up to 58 times more response, as compared to choosing the worst of the above parameters.

Channels of Direct Marketing

Any channel that can be used to deliver a message to a customer can be used in direct marketing, including:

1. Email marketing

Email marketing is one of the most commonly used direct-marketing methods. One reason for email marketing's popularity is that it is comparatively cheap to design, test, and send an email message. It also allows marketers to deliver messages around the clock, and to measure responses correctly.

2. Online tools

With the expansion of digital technology and tools, direct marketing is happening increasingly through online channels. Most online advertising is delivered to a focused group of customers and has a trackable response.

Display Ads are interactive ads that appear on the Web next to content on Web pages or Web services. Formats comprise static banners, pop ups, videos, and floating units. Customers can click on the ad to answer the message or to find more information.

Search: Whenever a potential customer enters a related search term, ads are allowed to be delivered to customers on the basis of their already-indicated search criteria. Marketers also use search engine optimisation to drive traffic to their sites.

Social Media Sites, such as Facebook and Twitter, also provide opportunities for direct marketers to correspond directly with customers by forming a content to which customers can reply.

3. Mobile

Through mobile marketing, marketers connect with potential customers and donors in an interactive way through a mobile device or network, such as a cell phone, smart phone, or tablet. Types of mobile marketing messages include: *SMS & MMS*. Marketing communications are sent in the form of media messages. Smartphone-based mobile apps have many kinds of messages like Push Notifications, *Location-Based Marketing, QR Codes* (quick-response barcodes) *Mobile Banner Ads.*

4. Telemarketing

Telemarketing is another common form of direct marketing, in which marketers contact customers by phone. The main benefit to companies is increased lead generation, which assists companies in increasing sales volume and customer base. The most successful telemarketing service providers concentrate on generating more "qualified" leads that have a higher prospect of being changed into actual sales.

5. Voicemail marketing

Voicemail marketing emerged from the market popularity of personal voice mailboxes, and business voicemail systems. Voicemail marketing was a cost effective means to reach people directly, by voice. In recent times, businesses have used guided voicemail (an application where pre-recorded voicemails are guided by live callers) to achieve personalised business-to-business marketing previously reserved for telemarketing.

Voice-mail courier is the same form of voice-mail marketing with both business-to-business and business-to-consumer applications.

6. Broadcast faxing

Broadcast faxing, in which faxes are sent to multiple recipients, is now less common than in the past. Around 2 percent of direct marketers use fax, mostly for business-to-business marketing campaigns.

7. Couponing

Couponing is used in print and digital media to draw out a response from the reader. An example is a coupon which the reader gets through the mail and takes to a store's check-out counter to get a discount.

Digital Coupons: Manufacturers and retailers sell coupons online for electronic orders that can be downloaded and printed. Digital coupons are available on company websites, social media outlets, texts, and email alerts. There is a growing number of mobile phone applications offering digital coupons for direct use.

Daily Deal Sites offer local and online deals each day, and are becoming more and more famous. Customers sign up to get notice of discounts and offers, which are sent daily by email. Purchases are frequently made using a special coupon code or promotional code.

3.2.6 Advertising

Advertising is the most famous channel of delivering messages to customers and prospective customers. The reason for advertising is to persuade customers that a company's services or products are the best, improve the image of the firm, show and create a need for products or services, show new uses for established products, announce new products and programs, support the salespeople's individual messages, attract customers to the company and to hold existing customers.

Almost any channel can be used for advertising. Commercial advertising media can comprise of wall paintings, billboards, street furniture components, printed flyers and rack cards, radio, cinema and television adverts, web banners, mobile telephone screens, shopping carts, web pop-ups, skywriting, bus stop benches, human billboards and forehead advertising, magazines, newspapers, town criers, sides of buses, banners attached to or sides of airplanes ("logo jets"), in-flight advertisements on seatback tray tables or overhead storage bins, taxicab doors, roof mounts and passenger screens, musical stage shows, subway platforms and trains, elastic bands on disposable diapers, doors of bathroom stalls, stickers on apples in supermarkets, shopping cart handles (grabertising), the opening section of streaming audio and video, posters, and the backs of event tickets and supermarket receipts.

Any place an "identified" sponsor pays to deliver their message through a channel is advertising.

Advertising for example, a billboard promoting a brand concept or product awareness—while seen by the customer, does not call for a specific response, and therefore cannot be easily measured. A marketer doesn't know exactly how effective such a billboard is, or how many people are thinking about and buying the product because of the billboard. However, because of the specific call to action, he or she does know exactly how many people responded to a direct mailing.

Various competing models of hierarchies of effects attempt to provide a theoretical underpinning to advertising practice.

- The model of Clow and Baack clarifies the objectives of an advertising campaign and for each individual advertisement. The model postulates six steps a buyer moves through when making a purchase:
    1. Awareness
    2. Knowledge
    3. Liking
    4. Preference
    5. Conviction
    6. Purchase
- Means-End Theory suggests that an advertisement should contain a message or means that leads the consumer to a desired end-state.

3.3 ACTIVITIES IN EVENT MANAGEMENT

In events, activities generally differ with the category of event being organised. Thus, the following listing is general in nature. We will first take a look at the flow of work for an event. We shall then understand the nature of staffing needed and some common names in an event management company and the reporting skill that an event manager requires to have. The organising and planning processes that are required to be followed for the successful completion of an event will then follow.

Once marketing has managed to change an enquiry into a firm order, the hands-on work of event management starts. The following is a sequential flow of how management actually comes about, that is, how planning, organising, staffing etc. gel together for an event. The flow is segregated into three sections – the first deals with the pre-event activities, the second with the during-event activities and the last details the post-event activities involved.

We shall now move on to activities involved in the event management flow. It is significant to note that we have followed a chronological sequencing of activities and not separated them with regards to work content. This has been done so as to introduce a sense of timing of the activities regarding one another. This is required so as not to lose sight of the woods for the trees.

3.3.1 Pre-event Activities

The number of activities required to prepare an event before the event occurs, wouldn't be anywhere near infinity. There are only so many limited activities; of course, the pre-event activities surpass the during- and post-event activities with regards to both significance and quantum. We have identified more than fifty such tangible discernible steps which are discussed here. These steps are essentially an addition of the 5 C's of events.

1. Events generally have a team-based work environment and a project type of organisation structure. Therefore, responsibilities are allotted to the related staff employees in the team for the event.

2. Co-ordination of the arrangements required is divided among the team members. Once the initial discussions are over, and the final concept sold to the client, the very first step starts when the creative conceptualiser works on the brief with the creative team.

3. A brief is a detailed list of input and specific instructions from the client for the event. Then the project manager prepares a thorough schedule after understanding the important steps and issues involved in that specific event.

4. External agencies such as architects and engineering contractors are consulted at this phase to understand the possibility of planned ideas. Most event management firms have experienced production managers who know the feasibility of a concept with total practical experience and it is not necessary for them to have exposure to special education.

5. Then the project manager draws up a cash flow statement, a budget statement and arranges budget allocation for the event. The information is updated and then facilitates correct budget forecasts for venue hire, construction of sets, special effects, lighting and sound etc.

6. It is important that in the absence of rate contracts with other networking elements, the event management firm updates itself with the existing market rates of the abovementioned important components before committing on any particular creative.

7. On the basis of the project requirements, critical dates or deadlines are drawn up and the best possible solution among options to attain these deadlines is selected. As a result of the deadlines, co-ordination of responsibilities is once again assessed with due consideration for contingency circumstances.

8. It is important that at this point, the overall co-ordinator connections with the client for support on the progress of the project dismissing doubt, explaining patiently and sharing views on the event.

9. The overall co-ordinator together with the sales and marketing team must guarantee the completion of overall designs, models of stage, visuals, etc. with graphics included by the creative team within the stipulated deadlines and make a researched concept presentation to the customer.

10. At this stage, the legalities of preparing the contract, agreements and finalisation by signing of contracts between the event managers and customers becomes a requirement. Contracts with customers and suppliers including penalty clauses and deadlines are then jointly confirmed by signing related contracts.

11. Ongoing budget control and supervision is conducted to observe deviations from the budget. Authorisation of payments to the suppliers as per the cash flow and contracts signed is the next rational step once the event is legally bound.

12. Committing to suppliers and then giving the payments a little late is a sure way to kill the firm given that the dependence on external agencies is very high in the events industry.

13. At the same time, working drawings need to be finished and printed for quotation from suppliers. Special effects are decided and briefs prepared for implementation.

14. Keeping the feasibility feature in mind, the finalisation of decisions concerning special effects is taken with the main contractors so that there is no communication gap and to guarantee correct practical outputs that can be expected.

15. Physical designs are then finalised and contractors start working. The purchase of event production material either on hire or loan is a common occurrence as stated above. Fire, safety and insurance issues need to be taken care of.

16. The co-ordinators and sales and marketing team are then kept busy keeping track of the progress made till date and arranging for catch-up plans. Simultaneously, event co-ordinators are required to supervise the contractors to guarantee that they are working with attention to detail for mounting special effects.

17. Supervising the contractors in workshops, having a discussion with the graphic designer for finalising illustrations and photographs and liaisoning with the client or clients' ad-agency on production of advertising promotions, support literature, brochures, posters, etc. are all significant recurring activities that the event co-ordinators need to track continuously.

18. Logistics is another significant area that needs to be given priority attention by event co-ordinators. Logistics in events basically involves booking of hotels, air, road and rail transport for the participants and event managers, arranging transportation of material which mostly weighs in tonnes and dealing with tax, Octroi and other government departments. At this stage, it is very important to keep the clients updated on the developments and progress to drive out fears, if nothing else.

19. Fire and safety measures to be double-checked and progress tracking and re-examining catch-up plans are some midway activities which are not of any value addition but guarantee that small sparks don't catch fire.

20. A joint team of the concept creation team and the main contractors then need to check out the special effects equipment and arrangements. It is now significant to maintain association with and oversee the special effects and electrical contractors.

21. Day by day tracking of timing and finance with a feedback on possible changes that is, rise or fall in expenditure on different items. A continuous surveillance of the cash flow is justified as liquidity needs are high and an expense once incurred is money expensed. And as events are mostly one-off in nature and unique, it is very important that investments in assets be examined.

22. On the production front again, completed art works by graphic designers are to be acquired and stored with care. Also, the production manager has to contact specialist producers, screen printers and colour processors for print media campaign and audio/video pictures for TV and radio promotions.

23. At this stage, finalisation of cleaning, security, furniture, decor (flowers), communication (telephones), and other service hire contracts (couriers) also take up the production manager's time.

24. The project manager handles the progress reporting and prepares contingency plans. The overall co-ordinator has to carry on co-operating with the client with reference to the PR, publicity, press releases, and promotions on TV, and radio together with the public relations team.

25. Arranging a press conference for the clients and artists, giving out invitations, passes and tickets to the event, organising the reception for the press with uniforms for the hospitality hostesses/hosts or staff at the reception is also a major responsibility for the public relation team in the preparatory stages leading up to the event.

26. Damage control because of artists' tantrums is yet another feature typical of this field that the public relation team needs to deal with. These have to be tolerated and controlled to avoid any adverse consequences.

27. Final visits for quality checks and control need to be made to the networking components to guarantee understandings and verify the same. The production

manager inspects the dimensions of stage and precision of models that are nearly finished.

28. The overall co-ordinator along with the other team members then needs to arrange for a briefing of site, supervising staff depending on the category and type of event. It is important that the complete briefing and communication take place before the event begins.

29. Once the event begins the clients and the contractors' employees' needs should not interfere with the implementation by the production manager and the event co-ordinators. Controlling the panic reactions because of invariable last minute hiccups and final tying up of all loose ends is a last significant task.

30. Organisation of the welcome reception, which is most frequently a very significant part of the event, is dictated by the understanding of the undercurrents in how this initial part of the event is laid out. A detail of VIP visits, security, toilets, etc. though apparently ignorable are however equally, if not more significant than the event itself. This is particularly true for political events.

31. The last stage in the first section includes resolution of on-site wrangles of delivery, permissions, missing orders or items, close attention to construction of sets – asking whether it was done right, supervision of installation of special effects, objects, low profile supervision of all site work and any extras agreed on-site and resisting emotional blackmail from the employees with regards to threats of walking out of the project by important employees.

3.3.2   During-event Activities

Unlike most other work profiles, events are unique in that most of the activities for an event are pre-event.

1. During the event, softer aspects come into focus. For the overall co-ordination, it is important to pass on all credit to supervisors.

2. Event managers should look modest and be available for the customer to call on. At least during the event, the hard work put in by the conceptualisers' should be appreciated. The fundamentals can be discussed later for improvements.

3. Simultaneously, there should be a constant surveillance of the special effects, display objects and the food and beverages.

4. Therefore, monitoring is the general idea of the during-event implementation activity that is involved.

5. Photographs and other multimedia recording arrangements if so required also need to be taken from strategic places.

3.3.3 Post-event Activities

Beginning with the physical task of dismantling of the sets, post-event activities also run into accounting and other such softer ins and outs that any firm, regardless of its field of operation, runs into.

1. Final account settling is accompanied by explanations for overspends.

2. The teams need to carry out a follow-up on the event, for example, in the form of a photo-documentary helps a lot. Performance assessment of the co-ordinators during the event should be conducted at once so that the stillness after the event can be used for learning.

3. Finally, the overall co-ordinator should thank all concerned for the extra efforts provided. Letters should go out to the customers thanking them and these should include a post-event questionnaire seeking to measure client satisfaction.

4. On the basis of this feedback, improvements and adjustments needed should be worked upon.

3.4 FUNCTIONS OF EVENT MANAGEMENT AS PER MANAGEMENT THEORY

As discussed above, the activities involved in event management can be further divided within the framework of contemporary conceptual developments in management. This will allow one to understand the importance of event management by building on the broad-based edifice of management theory. This theory says that the functions of management can be divided into planning, organising, staffing, leading, coordination and controlling.

3.4.1 Planning

A closer look at the planning function that the overall co-ordinator, the project manager and the sales team is dedicated to is justified here.

1. Planning tries to improve the usage of resource across the board. A cross-functional team is a necessity here given the difficulty in decision-making involved and the requirement for phenomenal researched data.

2. Starting with understanding the customer profile, the instructions for the event, the target audience and number expected, a major part of any event that follows is the preparation of the event cash flow statement.

3. Planning involves preparing the mission statements and goals on the basis of which strategies are devised to attain the set goals. Once the strategy is prepared, appropriate policies need to be created to align procedures and rules in order to be together with the strategy and allow – not hamper – the execution of the strategic

plan. Planning therefore tries to guarantee synergy in the decision-making process among the different activities.

4. The planning function is involved in micro-level event co-ordination activities such as communicating with the creative team discussing, facilitating and arranging for the technical specification, namely, sound, light, stages and sets. Short-listing artists and stand by artists in accord with the orders of the creative team is one of the most difficult tasks in the planning function.

5. It also involves checking out other arrangements for locating the event, the venue, the conditions for the event and collecting data to help in taking a decision on whether the event would be held indoors or outdoors. While at the last task, understanding the needs of licenses, clearances etc. and arranging for the same as and when needed is basically a task that the event co-ordinator is burdened with.

6. Deciding soft issues such as whether the show is to be ticketed, non-ticketed, completely or partly sponsored is also part of the planning exercise. Planners then do a risk rating for the event. Planning function includes deciding arrangements for the quality of hospitality and the dress code of the hosts/hostesses depending on audience profile plus deciding the suitable food and beverages to be served on the event. This is particularly so since the security and the other arrangements will differ with the kind of beverages served.

7. In the cash flow statements, inflows to the event company's coffers are essentially from a combination of the revenues from sponsorships, ticket sales, commissions, event production charges, artist management fees and infrastructure and equipment rental charges.

8. Simultaneously, on the outflow front, one can include headings as suppliers' payments, venue hiring charges, payment to artists and performers etc.

9. The major outflows though are mostly on the event production front joint with the licensing and tax payments liabilities. The mode of payment for event ranges from part payments to cash payments and is jointly agreed upon between the parties involved and authenticated in the form of a contract after negotiations.

10. Penalty clauses may also be included for non-payments. Depending on the nature of the project, the relationship with the customers and the goals of both the client and the organiser, the original plan of payments can be worked out. This may involve a specific amount as part payment in advance, a particular amount either at the commencement of the event or upon completion of the event. It is important that a specific amount be taken as advance to support the requirements of the working capital.

The planning function defines the limits of the creative function as it gives the restrictions that the creative team has to work with. It deals with practical realities for example, the logistics, that is, transportation of material, travel, stay etc. and the networking as media plan, ad designs, banners printing, tickets/ invites designing, and printing. It tries to form the perfect picture of the event flow and tries to define and control the inflow and outflow of money before, during and after the event. Thus, it is very important that the planning function plays a significant role in preparing any event. Besides that, the time-frame involved in decision-making being limited, planning presumes that much more significance as a function.

Some of the event planning services that are to be looked after by the event organisers are listed as follows – travel arrangements, audio-visual needs, catering, china and flatware, convention services, decor, decorations and props, entertainment, exhibitor needs, floor plan, food and beverages, ground transportation, invitations, linen, lodging, logistics, meeting planning, national entertainment, on-site co-ordination, on-site registration, photography, pipe and drape, registration, sanitation facilities, security, signage, site selection, sound and lights, speakers, stage decor, staging, tables and chairs, tenting, tours, union labour, valet, video production, staff, bar tenders, and website management.

3.4.2 Organising

As studied earlier, events usually have a team-based work environment and a project type of organisation structure and that responsibility is allotted to the related staff members in the team for the event. Co-ordination of the arrangements required is divided among the team members.

Understanding organising in the context of event management basically involves the description of the activities needed for an event, identifying individual and team tasks and distributing responsibilities to co-ordinators. Such an exercise assists in creating a clear structure of roles and positions. These structures change with almost every event depending upon the resources available. Thus, in management parlance, organisation structure in events is known as a project type of structure.

1. Event co-ordinators are basically needed for the organising part for an event.

2. Starting from getting in touch with the artist or performers and in case of absence, making arrangements for a substitute is one of the most significant functions of the event co-ordinator.

3. After planning and creative functions have worked out the game plan, the event co-ordinator then goes about fixing the date, terms and conditions with the artist. This is followed by arranging and creating necessary infrastructure.

4. Planning and synchronising with the professionals for the physical availability of the sound, lights, stage, sets and seating is followed by arranging for some softer features of organising.

5. These involve handling the publicity, which includes press meets, releases etc. for a favourable coverage and handling of ticketing and invitations.

6. The actual procurement of permissions and licenses from different Government departments ultimately becomes the co-ordinator's responsibility once the planning stage determines the requirements.

7. Arranging for hospitality such as the stay, food and beverages, hostesses, etc. and getting in touch with sponsors to guarantee fulfillment of commitments from the event organisers' side to their clients are part of the organising function. Briefly, organising is making the event happen within the limits defined by planning.

At this point in time, it would be sensible if the staffing requirements for events are introduced.

3.4.3 Staffing

Functional responsibilities in a project type organisation structure define event management staffing requirements. The significance of team structure, experience, background and expertise of team members plays an important role in event management. It is the size and the availability of resource in the events that to a certain degree defines the exact role of the staff members.

In a big company, there is more scope for specialised functional employees with limited functional responsibilities, whereas, in a small company, there is a fusion of roles depending simply on availability of time and staff. People friendly and savvy professionals are required to man this post on the event front. Therefore, while recruiting for events, one tends to feel that candidates with a past background in the hospitality industry, sales and advertising is preferred to tackle the stress and pumped up adrenaline level that come free with events.

The events that are mentioned before are very physical in nature. A group of skilled and unskilled volunteers and labour staff need to be directed efficiently. Given the fact that events are do or die projects, that is, are one-off in nature, trouble shooting in and during the event thus demands the most street smart and event savvy individuals.

Functionally, one can separate the following functional level responsibilities that need to be addressed within the team for a particular event as discussed above in the organising.

1. The co-ordinator is the person responsible for a specific event. He has the final authority in decision-making matters connected to the event.

2. The creative manager leads the creative team.

3. The project manager's role is to create a successful event and plays a very significant role in the planning function.

4. The production managers are also involved from the planning stage though their main responsibility is to make a successful event.

5. Sales and Marketing employees are part of the team from negotiating with future clients to guarantee the client-concept fit for the event right through to the execution of the event.

6. At most event firms, business development is also part of the marketing portfolio of activities.

7. Event co-ordinators carry the responsibility of everyday liaison and micro level activities. Event co-ordinators are the ones who do a lot of hard work and put the pieces together. They also need to be familiar with public relations activities and people skills in handling volunteers for putting up banners, décor etc.

8. Also, they need to be technically skilful as they shall be guiding the technical staff (sound, light, stages etc.) plus a host of skilled and experienced labour (carpenters, electricians, etc.) and unskilled labour (helpers) without whom there just cannot be any event.

3.4.4 Leading and Co-Ordination

The event altogether revolves around interpersonal skills. The need for attaining synergy among individual efforts so that the team goal is reached is the main objective of co-ordination. In general, the co-ordinators need to be leaders and are required to have good people skills. They are constantly required to encourage the labour and other junior co-ordinators to put more efforts given the physical nature of the job, the time constraints involved and the one-off nature of the event. The co-ordinator also should be capable of guiding the marketing and project managers and this includes passing on the experience and expertise of past events to relative new comers given the lack of professional event managers. Therefore, great communication skills and patience without letting too many mistakes happen plus knowing how to use the carrot and the stick in a balanced manner are the basic features of the co-ordinator. Other than the above, the leadership qualities required in an event manager include the ability to spot a deal and improvise.

3.4.5 Controlling

Controlling includes Evaluation and correction of differences in the event plans to guarantee consistency with original plans. Evaluation is an activity that seeks to know and calculate the extent to which an event has succeeded in attaining its goal. The purpose of an event will vary regarding the category and variation of event. On the other hand, to provide reach and interaction would be a general purpose that events fulfil.

There can be two attitudes with which evaluation can be put in its correct viewpoint. The concept of evaluation mentioned above was an important examination to discover what went wrong. A more productive focus for evaluation is to make suggestions about how an event might be improved to attain its goals more efficiently. To carry out an evaluation and measurement exercise, it is important that the predefined objectives of the events have been correctly understood. The brief should contain all the information to be communicated since if an event is organised without a proper reason then, any evaluation of it would be rather useless. The basic evaluation process in events involves three steps, namely, establishing tangible goals and incorporating sensitivity in evaluation, measuring the performance before, during and after the event, and finally correcting deviations from plans.

3.5   EVENT MANAGEMENT INFORMATION SYSTEM

Event management involves applying project management practices to designing, planning and co-ordinating special events such as parties, fund raisers, sporting activities and other affairs. Depending on the size of the event, information systems are used to track employees and resources.

An event management information system is designed to facilitate tracking employees and resources needed for running events. Normally, its main purpose is to provide scheduling and registration support. Additionally, other functions allow matching personnel needs to event staffing availability. The system also tracks costs and expenses. After the event, the system generates reports for administrative employees. Event management information systems allow planners to utilise processes and technology to co-ordinate activities that bring about a well-run event.

Features

Utilising specialised software and hardware to manipulate information using certain processes, event management information systems give event managers the data they require to maintain a competitive business edge. Event management information systems support organising entertainment, personal or corporate activities. Scalable systems enable one to plan, market and sell an event. In other words, despite there being a big or small a conference party, utilising an event management information system will assist in planning and running it.

Benefits

Automating the registration process using an event management information system decreases mistakes, saving time and money in addition. Managing donations online increases the probability of contributions. Mechanisms for generating newsletters and other online communication provide a lost-cost and environmentally friendly way of reaching an extensive audience, increasing participation. On the whole, event management information systems enable one to update communications and decrease operating costs.

A basic Event Management Information System (EMIS) needs to contain information concerning the following

1. **General Event Information:** Event category ID, event variation ID, name, type ID, status, location, the start date/time, end date/time, required staffing, confirmations, available spaces, event description in brief and the employee ID of the event managers.

2. **Event Attendees:** Attendee ID, first/last name, title, company name, address, phone/fax/email, website URL.

3. **Event Registration:** Registration ID, attendee ID, employee ID, event category ID, event variation ID, registration date/time, sales tax rates, fee schedule ID, Registration fee.

4. **Event Category:** Event category ID, event variation ID.

5. **Employees and Staff assigned to the Event:** Employee ID, name, title, phone/fax/email.

6. **Event Pricing:** Fee schedule ID, event ID, fee description, fee.

7. **Event Management Company Information:** Set up ID, sales tax rate, company name, address, phone/fax/email, default payment terms, default invoice description.

8. **Payment Records:** Payment ID, registration ID, payment amount/date, payment mode (credit card- name/expiry date/cheque/cash), payment method ID.

9. **Payment Methods:** Payment method ID, payment method, Debit/ATM card and Credit card.

This system should be capable of generating queries such as the number attendees at any given event, the total payments, and total registrations by an attendee etc. Reports that must be available from this system are: attendee listings, invoices, sales by employee, and event type.

The identity numbers are used to clearly differentiate between items and are generally only one of its kinds and generated by the system automatically. It keeps track of related records such that there is no repetition and duplication of entries plus keeping a chronological record of related fields such as attendees, and registrations etc, ID's help in maintaining and generating records. This framework is extended to be a web-based system that can be accessed from any computer everywhere, thus, giving greater control over information about the status of the event because of real time availability.

Finally, the value of focused databases of information obtained from the audience is an important asset for the event organisers and their customers. Such information in the form of organised databases can be very beneficial when sold as a product. A web-based B2B portal on the lines of a yellow pages service for event suppliers (B2B e-commerce) that maintains a web-based active database containing names, contact numbers, addresses, rates, etc. would be very beneficial to the event organiser. Every transaction generated with that supplier through the web shall be a chance, generated by the event organiser for the supplier. Therefore, there can be a contract-fee for maintaining data on the website. Allowing access to potential customers to this database would allow the client, particularly the corporate ones, to have more trust on the organiser and trust is a major part of the events business. Similar web-based services directly to individual clients can be established as a B2C engine.

3.6 TECHNOLOGY IN EVENT MANAGEMENT : ROLE & IMPORTANCE

The technology – with the important caveat of when it is used properly – is adding significantly to every area within our events. We see it playing a supporting role, through the cell or tablet, in amplifying the content within via social media. Technology helps our participants to be more interactive through hand held devices; be that paddles for voting, bump technology for networking or RFID chips for tracking their every move. We also see technologies tentacles reach into the rooms where we hold our events. Wires and cables transport content, through live or recorded feeds, into geographical areas we could otherwise never even dream of hoping to reach. The technology has four major roles in supporting the events industry and each area is of equal importance:

1. using technology to report back to stakeholders, clients or their managers,
2. using software to share information on the progress of tasks across the team,
3. using software to make budget automatically populated by actual income and expenditure,
4. using technology in a structured way so that the work could be easily replicated and risk assessed by their stakeholder, clients, managers or by themselves.

The technology has to be used to help organisers: it can move them away from the time consuming administrative tasks to really adding value. As well as improving our events, using technology also has one other major benefit: we appear much more professional. Attendee engagement, hybrid/web casting, amplification of their event, and helping manage and support their events are the four areas requested by clients to use the technology.

The technology has a crucial role in supporting the credibility of organizers and owing to this the use of technology has to be championed by the industry. It will surely add professionalism in our events. We have to use it as a way to demonstrate our understanding and control of our events. We need to use it as a structure to help us avoid mistakes and deliver better events. Events can be successfully planned, executed and reviewed without the use of technology. However, there are affordable technology solutions that can ease the burden and provide enhanced situational awareness during the event. If you are using the technology solution to help in securing your event, it is significant to keep in mind a few key points

- Do your homework – investigate, prepare and implement. Take time to evaluate your exact deliverables and what are you going to be held responsible for. Evaluating your deliverables and needs goes beyond the obvious: How are you going to manage and archive e-mails, meetings, conversations, images and plans? Executing correct technology solution will help you in this process and provide your staff with less administrative burdens found in planning big scale events.

- Don't just choose technology, choose a technology partner. Planning an event is an energetic task. Ensure that the firm you select is ready to understand your business processes and helps you in adapting technology with your most challenging issues.

- Don't learn your technology during a crisis. Choose a technology solution that is very user-friendly.

When securing an event, everyone works toward the same goal: An event where people do not think twice about security. The right technology solution can quickly put more correct data in the hands of those who need it and enable people to concentrate on their mission, not on paperwork.

Uses of Information Technology for Events

1. Areas of event planning and control that can benefit from IT

 ➢ Scheduling

 ➢ Financial control and Budgeting

 ➢ Promotion

- ➢ Distribution
- ➢ Control and reporting
- ➢ Risk management and scenario building
- ➢ Contact management
- ➢ Site/venue layout
- ➢ Staffing and volunteer management
- ➢ Vendor database management

Possible limitations of IT for events

- ➢ Financial costs
- ➢ Retraining staff
- ➢ Limited access, passwords and computer security
- ➢ Information loss
- ➢ Refocusing the event
- ➢ Software compatibility
- ➢ Restructuring the event company - particularly corporate culture problems and power shifts as a result of knowledge and skill ownership

Use of information software in

(a) Design stage

- ➢ Presentation software such as PowerPoint
- ➢ Spreadsheet software to establish budget scenarios such as Excel and Lotus, CAD
- ➢ Graphics software in the creation of themes and logos, studio max, corel draw, photoshop etc.

(b) Planning process and basic business support

- ➢ Word processing packages such as MS Word and Word Perfect
- ➢ Accounting software packages such as Quicken, MYOB, spreadsheets
- ➢ Project management software including MS Project
- ➢ Data management software including Dbase and Outlook
- ➢ Communication software including Eudora and MS Outlook

(c) Marketing of the event

- ➢ Ticketing and smart card use
- ➢ Tracking
- ➢ Internet marketing and websites

(d) Implementation

- ➢ Registration in both sport and conference software
- ➢ Audio visual software
- ➢ Video production and editing software
- ➢ CDROM production
- ➢ Digital broadcast
- ➢ Scoring and scoreboard display (electronic, LCD, CED, Manna')

2. Implementation of a computer system for an event

Evaluation and control procedures for the IT

- ➢ Vendor stability and expert availability
- ➢ Software support
- ➢ Repair and maintenance
- ➢ Backups
- ➢ Upgrading
- ➢ Report and report distribution

Considerations in implementation of a computer system for an event

- ➢ User licensing
- ➢ Training staff and volunteers
- ➢ Operating, a pilot system
- ➢ Running a parallel system
- ➢ Phase in/Phase out system
- ➢ Cut off method

Points to Remember

- Promotion in events is required to get the desired reach. Networking components like print media, radio, television, internet, cable network, and the outdoor media, which are involved in the process of promotion.
- The pre-event publicity, which aids in increasing reach while the post-event coverage falls under the purview of journalism.
- Decision-making on using the print media essentially revolves around the variety of publications available, their circulation, the frequency of publication, whether weekly/daily/morning/evening, and the profile of readers.

- The programme profile, listening audience profile and time slots for airing the commercials are the major decision making criteria for Radio.

- The television media can be the single most potent media since it can provide pre-event, during event and post-event coverage.

- Multimedia integrates the print, audio and video media.

- The internet is now extensively used in events for online registration for events, dispensing information – both pre and post-event, in the form of databases, carrying out complex analysis of information obtained, providing opportunities related to e-commerce.

- The cable network is a medium and is most beneficial for a highly localised reach and coverage of events - the live as well as deferred coverage, growing rapidly in popularity.

- The low rates of advertising on the cable network media is also an involving networking with the cable channels is normally based on the localities that the channel covers and number of cable connected homes.

- Prime locations, size and number of hoardings, posters and banners are the main decisions to be taken when planning outdoor media.

- Hoardings usually carry only broad event awareness messages and are designed for a relatively larger reach than banners and posters.

- Press conferences, press relations, invites to events for impresarios are some means of networking for good public relations.

- Event specific merchandising can be used for publicity before, during and after the event.

- Events have traditionally offered opportunities for successfully encashing on the merchandising opportunities that get generated. T-shirts based on the colours of popular teams or carrying pictures of star performers, toys and electronic games based on the event are few examples of such opportunities.

- The visibility, size and location of the sponsors' in-venue signage are essential for publicity during the actual event.

- Logos, banners, posters and handouts in and around the venue are designed to deliver the promises made for the event. They act as guides for the audience during the show. Special banners highlight contests inviting participation in various activities.

- Lester Wunderman is considered to be the father of contemporary direct marketing.

- Direct marketing messages involve a specific "call to action," such as "Call this toll-free-number" or "Click this link to subscribe." The results of such campaigns are immediately trackable and measurable, as a business can track responses, results and cost from prospects and/or customers, regardless of medium.

- The purpose of advertising is to convince customers that a company's services or products are the best, enhance the image of the company, point out and create a need for products or services, demonstrate new uses for established products, announce new products and programs, reinforce the salespeople's individual messages, draw customers to the business, and to hold existing customers.

- Any place an "identified" sponsor pays to deliver their message through a medium is advertising.

- Event management activities are in sequential flow which is divided into three sections – the first deals with the pre-event activities, the second with the during-event activities and the last details the post-event activities involved.

- Pre-event activities are basically an extension of the 5 C's of the event.

- During-event Activities, it is important to pass on all credit to supervisors, for the overall co-ordination. Event managers should look humble and be available for the client to call on.

- There is need of constant surveillance of the special effects, display objects and the food and beverages. Thus, monitoring is the gist of the during-event execution activity.

- Post-event Activities include follow-up, feedback, evaluation and correction that is, improvements and adjustments.

- The management theory states that the functions of event management can also be classified into planning, organising, staffing, leading and controlling.

- Planning ensures synergy in the decision making process among the various activities. It optimises resource utilisation across the board. It defines the limits of the creative function as it provides the constraints that the creative team has to work with.

- Understanding organising in the context of event management essentially involves the description of the activities required for an event, identifying individual and team tasks and distribution of responsibilities to co-ordinators.

- Some softer aspects of organising involve handling the publicity, which includes press meets, releases etc. for a favourable coverage and handling of ticketing and invitations. In short, organising is making the event happen within the constraints defined by planning.

- Events being 'do or die' projects demand the most street smart and event savvy individuals.

- Co-ordination achieves synergy among individual efforts so that the team goal is reached.

- Evaluation and correction of deviations in the event plans to ensure conformity with original plans is the gist of controlling.

- A basic Event Management Information System (EMIS) needs to contain information concerning the following: 1. General Event Information, 2. Event Attendees, 3. Event Registration, 4. Event Category, 5. Employees and Staff assigned to the Event, 6. Event Pricing, 7. Event Management Company Information, 8. Payment Records, 9. Payment methods.

- The basic framework can be expanded to be a web-based system that can be accessed from any computer anywhere. Thus, giving greater control over information about the status of the event due to real time availability.

- The technology has a crucial role in supporting the credibility of organizers.

Questions for Discussion

1. Explain the various networking components of promotion of events to get the desired reach.

2. Describe the importance of well-planned PR activities.

3. What are the various opportunities for merchandising with respect to the events?

4. Explain in brief how the activities in event management are classified?

5. "Management theory can be applied to the activities in event management." Elaborate.

6. What is the significance of EMIS and what type of information is required for it?

7. What is strategic market planning? Describe the criteria for setting objectives for strategic market planning.

8. Which parameters need to be evaluated while assessing the market attractiveness?

9. Explain how business strengths are to be judged.

Chapter 4...

Marketing of Events

Contents ...

Learning Objectives ...

After going through this chapter, you will be able to gain an insight into the following

- To know about the market and distinct type of customers for events.

- To study segmentation and targeting of the market for events.

- To learn about positioning and branding in events with the concept of event property.

- To study the characteristics of different categories of events.

- To understand the important factors in pricing of events.

- To study the relative importance of events as a marketing communication tool.

- To be able to find out the diverse marketing needs addressed by events.

4.1   INTRODUCTION

Marketing of events aims at selling the events and making profits. Any successful event achieves the desired profits and other benefits like creating goodwill, brand building etc. Huge revenue is generated in the event industry. The very important and unique feature of the event industry is the interdependence of the various components that form this industry wherein the ownership of event infrastructure itself becomes a source of revenue for the event marketer. The most fundamental aspect is the event infrastructure and the core benefits attached with each of the event categories. Similarly, an event should meet both the tangible and intangible needs and aspirations of the event user satisfactorily. Most events are tailor-made or customised for the particular client depending on the requirements from the event and the objectives set to be met by the event as agreed between the event organiser and the client, as different event categories satisfy a variety of needs on different scales.

4.2 CONCEPT OF MARKET IN EVENTS

"A market consists of all the potential customers sharing a particular need or want who might be willing and able to engage in exchange to satisfy that need or want." – defines Philip Kotler, a marketing guru.

In events, there are two distinct types of customers – customers from whom there is revenue generated for the event organiser and non-revenue generating customers.

4.2.1   Revenue Generating Customers

Revenue generating customers are the customers from whom the event organiser receives money for organising an event from these customers. Revenue generating customers are classified primarily into two categories, clients and target audience. Clients need events for marketing communications whereas the target audience need events to satisfy the need for entertainment, recreation, knowledge, etc. Event organisers satisfy the varied needs of the customers by carrying out events as desired by them.

Clients: The clients include the institutions, corporate houses, media houses etc. as mentioned below.

1. **Institutions:** Institutions involved or participating in the leisure industry such as clubs, motels and tourism promotion agencies require events that attract more customers for the activities and services that they offer. Institutions involved or taking part in sports and other competitive events have the most organised and well-structured governing devices amongst all event groups. Thus, for event organisers, these represent a tangible client to approach.

2. **Corporate houses and other institutions:** Corporates have a need for organising both external as well as internal events. External events for consumer-restricted products given the legal angle mean that such corporates use big events to satisfy their communication agenda. External events for consumer durable products use events to keep away from clutter on the traditional media and for many other reasons. Such events can also be organised for firms in the consumer non-durable sector. Internal events also at times need event organisers for professional execution. An internal event such as an annual general meeting is basically a low budget affair that is implemented in-house. Associations/industry forums connected to promotion of trade, culture need active organised events for numerous purposes.

3. **Media houses:** Press, television and the radio media owners also need events for general reasons, for example, software creations. Although big media houses are a

part of the industry, they also need events for certain communication campaigns for their services and products and thus are a part of the customer group for event organisers.

4. **Target audience:** The target audience is the final customer for the event who actually takes part in the event. If the event is a ticketed one, then the person taking part might be the buyer of the ticket. The target audience could also include invitees or the public. These are the most significant lot of revenue generating customers for the event marketers plus their customers. This is so because ticket buyers are direct revenue generators whereas invitees and the general public are indirect revenue earners in that the customers pay for their presence at the event. The clients rely on the indirect revenue earners for word-of-mouth publicity.

4.2.2 Non-revenue Generating Customers

Non-revenue customers are the customers besides the above important customers. There are many other entities that are required to be serviced or treated like a customer in the changed business scenario that needs one to be market-oriented whether there is a direct advantage of money or not. Indirect customers who predominantly are the most active carriers of word-of-mouth policy and do not necessarily generate a monetary gain for the event organisers should also be looked after properly. Thus, any entity that needs expending time and effort and which contributes to the successful execution of an event should also be treated as a customer in this business.

Influencers: Businessmen, ambassadors, foreign embassy officials etc. are customers who need to be cultivated for their potential to influence future clients in favour of a certain event agency.

Advertising agencies: Here events are organised for their clients in tandem in a specific media campaign. Ad agencies are also involved with events in that they are always needed to design and execute the publicity campaign for their customers who are using the services of an event agency for any event.

Regulatory bodies: Regulatory bodies such as government stakeholders who are non-revenue customers have to be given the same importance as any paying customer. Regulatory bodies as customers have a say in the success of the event and need to be serviced with a lot of patience and care. Revenue is generated from these customers in different forms such as sponsorships, charity and sales of tickets.

From this, one can see that the range of customers covered by events in its purview is great. The customers' requirement for a desired goal from events as a communication channel varies, therefore, giving rise to a need for a focused approach of first defining and targeting core customer groups.

4.3   SEGMENTATION AND NICHE MARKETING FOR EVENTS

The event can only be successful if there is right segmentation and targeting of customers, like all other products or services. The success of the client-concept-audience fit depends on the right segmentation of the market and then targeting a specific target segment. The event organisers must first segment clients and on this basis, continue segmentation of target audience. On the basis of their attractiveness, targeting of clients is done.

4.3.1   Segmentation

A market segment is a big group of customers within a market. As different customers – both clients and the target audience – vary in terms of different features, it is difficult to customise the communication to reach a person. The need for segmenting the market on the basis of broad features that comprise the market also emerges in order to reach a compromise between mass marketing and individual marketing by event organisers.

An example of mass marketing events is any ticketed show such as a cricket match wherein tickets for watching the game are sold to anybody on a first-come-first-served basis. In such events, sponsorship is open to the highest bidding customers. In case of mass marketing, the event is designed first and then is opened for any customer. Individual marketing in events is also called as customised events. These include designing a concept appropriate for a client and its customers, that is, the target audience.

Market segmentation is a very challenging job since event organiser needs to segment the market regarding both the client as well as the target audience to guarantee the client-audience fit. The segmentation of the market can be conducted based on the core concept preferences of the customers plus those of the target audience. The target audience can be segmented on the basis of standard demographic, geographic, economic and psychographic traits. In that segmentation of the target audience becomes very significant, they define which customers to approach for funding the events as well as event category and variation that the event organiser should concentrate on. Segmentation of clients is very significant as not only is the information on the brands, products or services of the customer significant but also the target audience that the client is going to attract is also very significant.

Benefit segmentation can be used for segmentation of clients. Segmentation on the basis of the benefits provided by events at the different levels that of, reach and communication can be called as benefit segmentation. Thus, clients can be segmented into clients seeking high reach with less interaction, equal reach and interaction or low reach with high interaction. Each of the event differences could also be changed into tangible event market segments.

Therefore, market segmentation for event organisers includes knowing which target audience and which client to serve simultaneously. Segmentation of the events market helps to identify the synergies between the target audience and the customer. This suffices for a certain extent in guaranteeing the client-concept-audience fit.

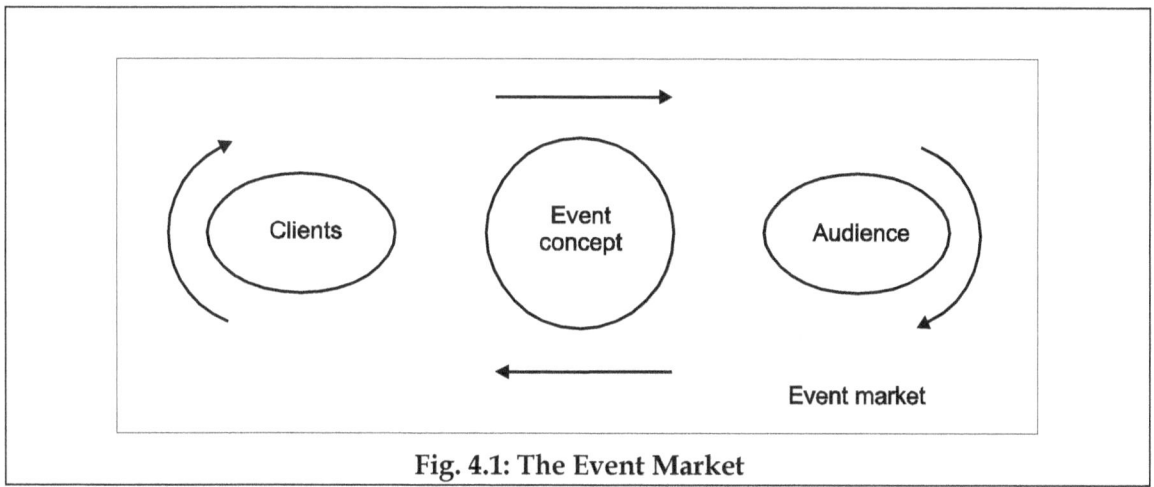

Fig. 4.1: The Event Market

Fig. 4.1 shows that the event market is made up of many big clients and audience. The concept can be changed and applied to any combination. It is up to the event organiser to define the segments and change their event concept accordingly.

4.3.2   Niche Marketing in Events

Event organisers prefer to concentrate on a niche area within a selected market segment such as concentrating on only cricket or football as the niche event in the competitive events group or only on music-related events in the artistic expression group of events. By catering to particular events and limiting their focus of clients and target audience, event organisers can try to satisfy the needs of a smaller sub-segment within a market segment whose requirements are not being well-served.

4.4   TARGETING

Once the market segments have been defined, it is essential that the event organiser chooses one or more of these segments to enter, consolidate and grow. To do this, assessment of each segment as to its attractiveness is important. It is also necessary that event organisers work on the targeting problem based on their goals and resources.

Attractiveness of a segment can be calculated indirectly for financial benefits and influence with regards to the potential reach and scope for interaction that the segment gives. The greater the reach and interaction, the greater the attractiveness for clients and therefore, bigger the size, growth, profitability, scale economies and so on of the segment for the event organiser. Such segments also guarantee lesser risks for the event organisers. The targeting decision also depends on other considerations like ease with which members of the segment can be won over. Clients who were unhappy with the services provided by other event organisers should also be highly considered. The clients' business value in terms of event-spend in the event category that the organiser is interested in, loyalty and ability to control other clients is also a significant part of the decision-making for targeting clients.

Next, the event organisers should examine their goals and resources and think whether investing in the segment is in synergy with these. That is, the event organisers' interests, skills and long-term objectives, which determine the event categories that it will serve, must be similar to the requirements of the segment. If the event organiser lacks one or more necessary competencies and is in no position to get them, the segment will automatically get scratched from the options available. A major help in targeting a segment however, is the ability to develop some greater advantages for a specific segment that other event organisers cannot get in the short term. Such segments where the event organiser can give superior value to the client are the most attractive ones.

In the easiest case, an event organiser can choose to select and work in a single segment. This carries a little more risk than normal and simultaneously the chance to get a strong knowledge of the segment's requirements. This can allow the event organiser to attain a strong place in the segment. The risk is high when the segment attractiveness declines, then the event organiser is left without any support or relief. There is also the possibility that competition may enter the segment in a big way affecting the attractiveness again. Therefore, most event organisers prefer to be there in more than one segment. These segments, each attractive and compatible with the event organisers' interests, may or may not have any harmony amongst them, though each segment should certainly be a monetary minefield. This leads to spreading the risks such that if one segment becomes monetarily unappealing, the other segments support the event organiser and keep the cash register ringing.

Another way of targeting includes event specialisation. The event organiser aspires to create a particular concept within an event category for catering to many segments. For instance, an event organiser concentrating only on music concerts and who does not bother about the other avenues for artistic expression would have different customers particularly interested in the event category. The event specialisation strategy may take a risk in losing clients to another event variation within the event category. In the market specialisation strategy, the event organiser can focus on satisfying the multiple needs of a specific customer group. This is a targeting strategy in which the event organiser provides a selected list of specific clients a number of services that may be from different event groups.

Through this, the event organiser creates a strong reputation for specialising in events for specific client industries. In matter of risks, a major risk here is that fluctuations in the clients' financial health may have an effect on the event organisers directly. On the better side, an improvement in the clients' fortunes may actually cause a boom time for the event organisers. By trying to serve the whole market, an event organiser shows the first signs of growing in size and height. Event organisers can serve the whole market by either ignoring the market segment differences or by acknowledging the differences and designing events for each segment.

The corporates, which are the clients for event organisers, on their parts, are unashamed about their goals. For instance, when it comes to college festivals – ambitious, brand-conscious students fit right into their target markets – be it for a toothpaste, website, paint or soap – and the festivals provide both simple and direct access to this audience. Even a Ford car dealer thinks that such gathering of college students of a specific age group makes a good event to sponsor. Event organisers should consider this factor when targeting clients.

4.5 POSITIONING IN EVENTS

After the segmentation and targeting it is then subjected to positioning which involves ascertaining how a product or a company is perceived in the minds of consumers, so as to develop the event as a property.

To establish and communicate the event, organisers' products, that is, events key benefits to the market is known as positioning. After the segmentation and targeting of the event market, each target segment then needs to be studied for possible positioning ideas. These are then selected, developed and communicated.

When the list of target markets is made, a company might want to start on deciding on a good marketing mix directly. But an important step before developing the marketing mix is deciding on how to create an identity or image of the product in the mind of the customer. Every segment is different from the others, so different customers with different ideas of what they expect from the product.

Once a market segment has been identified (via segmentation), and targeted (in which the viability of servicing the market intended), the segment is then subject to positioning. Positioning involves ascertaining how a product or a company is perceived in the minds of consumers.

This part of the segmentation process consists of drawing up a perceptual map, which highlights rival goods within one's industry according to perceived quality and price. After the perceptual map has been devised, a firm would consider the marketing communications mix best suited to the product in question.

4.6 BRANDING IN EVENTS: THE CONCEPT OF EVENT PROPERTY

What is brand in marketing language connected to consumer and industrial products can be called as event property in events marketing. Event property is that aspect of an event that separates the event from the limitations posed by canvassing. It creates an event concept that can be organised continuously using different artists and venues for different clients and target audiences.

It involves restraining degrees of freedom with which event can be conducted while simultaneously removing any restrictions from the path of the event moving towards a pre-planned affair year after year. Event property also has the feature that it belongs to the event organiser and cannot be taken away or stolen by competitors.

For instance, the Miss India pageant – a beauty and talent contest is the event conducted yearly regardless of the change in the contestants, judges, venues, clients and target audience, etc. Femina, a part of the Times of India Group, owns the event and its event property. The event property of the Miss India pageant is its official recognition as a national contest for selecting the Indian representatives for the Miss Universe, Miss World and Miss Asia Pacific contests. This makes it very hard and impossible for any competitor to steal the idea away.

4.7   REACH-INTERACTION MATRIX

The categories of events as given in 2.1.5 can be presented in the reach-interaction matrix according to their characteristics. The reach-interaction matrix gives the summary of the general features of each of the categories to allow a bird's eye-view on events. On the other hand, each category can be designed in such a way as to change the degree of reach and interaction.

		Reach	
		High	Low
Interaction	High	Special Business Exhibitions	Cultural
	Low	Competitive Artistic	Charitable

Table 4.1: Reach-Interaction Matrix

Amongst the different event groups corporate interests have focused on competitive events, particularly so on cricket in India. Such events have a broad-based character and high media coverage. This means high reach and the added excitement through live coverage on different famous channels. Post-event benefits of such events include event highlights, event recall and above the normal benefits. The fact that interaction is given unsympathetic dismissal is a peculiarity that needs to be corrected. Competitive events are closely followed by events for artistic expression, then by exhibitions, special business events, cultural and charitable events in that order for popularity with event-savvy sponsors.

In fact, according to the leading American advertising journal *Advertising Age,* corporate spending on events in America has increased by 17 percent per annum since the late 1980s. Events connected to sports top the list by cornering about 45 percent of the total event spending; music and art events symbolise a combined 35 percent billing. Rest of the event-spend is shared by the other event categories. In the same way, in Canada, almost 60 percent of the Canadian $500 corporate spending on events is on sporting events. The total event-spend in the United Kingdom is put at 12 million pounds. In the Indian context, industry watchers expect growth rates of 50-100 percent in the next five years and an event-spend in the region of Rs. 500 crores, therefore making this industry an attractive business.

The event infrastructure required for each event category can be summarised as shown below in Table 4.2. The underlying fundamental infrastructure of these event categories has been tabulated to understand the categorisation of events better.

Table 4.2: Category-wise Event Infrastructure

Event Category	Core Concept	Core People	Core Talent	Core Structure
Competitive	Challenge of skills and strategies between two or more entities	Sports-persons, athletes	Specific game(s)	Very organised
Artistic Expression	Expression of talent for entertainment	Musicians, dancers and other creative professionals	Artistic creativity and expertise	Professional circuits yet to be organised
Cultural Celebration	Get-togethers, joy	Performers and professionals of participating client organisations	Rituals and informality	Organised in individual communities
Exhibitions	Display and sale	Manufacturers, artists	Workman-ship	Very organised
Charitable	Making available for giving more than what one can	Philanthropists	A feeling, an urge to help and raise funds by using other core concepts	Not organised
Special Business	Making a difference for commercial gain	Celebrities, models, marketing professionals	Creative and marketing savvy	Highly disorganised

Though the grouping of events altogether might seem to be comprehensive, they are not unique in nature. An event can be a mix of the above groups too. For example, having an entertainment programme during or after a trade fair is almost a common occurrence. Categorising such a stage show separately, as an event here would not be correct as the reason for such a show to take place was the trade fair. But from the event organiser's viewpoint, this is a mixed matched account of two different groups of events that need different levels of skill and management input.

Therefore, each of the groups of events can be tailor made or merged to suit any of the marketing needs of the corporate sponsor. Combined with the possibilities in the networking plans and barter deals and others, the situation that emerges is one of having to decide amongst a huge number of changes and combinations that are technically practicable but difficult to implement in reality.

4.8   CONCEPT OF PRICING IN EVENTS

Each event, even within the same group and variation, will vary immensely in the manner it is priced, though particular production costs can be standardised. Another significant consideration in pricing of events is that the event organisers need to price the event separately for clients and target audience. Therefore, a close look should be taken at the pricing process in practice. A thorough knowledge of the pricing process will guarantee that related parts involved in reaching the magic figure are not ignored. A conscious effort in this direction will definitely bring about a genuine and reliable figure. Pricing in practice usually involves risk rating.

4.8.1   Risk Rating

The first step in pricing is to determine whether the event will be fully sponsored, partially sponsored and partially ticketed or fully ticketed. All the three options carry different levels of risk as indicated in the Table 4.3.

A decision on how much risk the event organiser is willing to take will lead towards understanding the scope of pricing as to whether the pricing is to be completed for clients or for pricing of tickets for the target audience.

Nature of Events	Level of Risk
Fully sponsored events	Least risk
Partially sponsored and partially ticketed events	Medium risk
Fully ticketed events	High risk

Table 4.3: Risk Rating

4.8.2 Setting Pricing Objectives in Tune with Marketing and Business Strategies

The different pricing alternatives that are available will depend on the corporate strategy and the marketing strategy accepted by the agency for its development. Since pricing is an important part of marketing, it follows then that the marketing strategy will dictate the strategic pricing objectives. Generally, the alternative goals may range from increasing margins from present events to increasing efficiency and simultaneously decreasing costs.

4.8.3 Feedback from the Market

In event business, the sources of feedback information are –

(i)   From market research of end customers for the event

(ii) From information on competitors

(iii) From friendly customers who tell you what they paid for previous events to your competitor

(iv) From published sources and general press such as magazine and newspapers – an estimate of the costs and pricing involved may be available through interviews or articles

(v)   Reports from the sales force

(vi) Feedback from lost orders

(vii) From talking to new employees, who join you from other firms

(viii) For government activities, tendering is frequently public and the results are available for study

Though the feedback available generally tends to give sufficient information, conversion into active information should be completed after considering the ethical practices and distortion of information. Experience alone can help to identify the direct importance of the data to the event pricing.

4.8.4 Skills Required for Negotiating the Best Price

(i)   Good communication and selling skills

(ii) Market research or intelligence gathering ability

(iii) Thorough knowledge of limitations and potential of creative concept and execution of event

(iv) Ability to take a quick decision as to the importance in money terms of a particular potential benefit that could be offered to the client during a negotiation

(v)   Ability to make decisions on the basis of financial assessments

These are the skills and competencies required for the introduction of market-based pricing

4.8.5 Validation against Pricing Objectives

Altogether, any objective has to be in tune with the strategic aims of the company. Objectives are basically a face given to the tactical moves that a company adopts. Thus, they need to be validated against the formal documented business plans, marketing or corporate strategy, the mission statement and the annual reports. A validation exercise will guarantee that there is synchronisation between the pricing strategy and other parts of the marketing strategy.

4.8.6 A Thorough Assessment of the Internal Systems and Overheads

For any system to be classified as good, the management processes in that system should be in order and be capable of processing data and provide information when required. This is because a lot of importance is given to marketing intelligence. Each and every bit of information should be connected to the source, the date on which it was incorporated, the date till which it will be valid and at last, the precision and limitations involved with the information.

4.9   LEGISLATION AND TAX LAWS

It would be practical, if not necessary, to know and incorporate information of all related legislation and laws before the pricing model is decided upon. Legislation tends to change so quickly that keeping up with them can be pretty difficult. Still, legislation concerning taxation, price fixing, discriminatory pricing, deception, etc. should be kept track of even though they may not be relating to the event as such. It would be helpful in knowing whether the client is on the right side of the law too.

4.10 RELATIVE IMPORTANCE OF EVENTS AS A MARKETING COMMUNICATION TOOL

Event management is considered as one of the strategic marketing and communication tools by companies of all sizes. From product launches to press conferences, companies create promotional events to help them communicate with clients and potential clients. They might target their audience by using the news media, hoping to generate media coverage which will reach thousands or millions of people. They can also invite their audience to their events and reach them at the actual event.

The relative importance of the events with other modes of marketing communication can be represented by a two-dimensional matrix as shown in Fig. 4.2 which positions the life cycle stages on the horizontal axis and the relative position of the tools on the vertical axis.

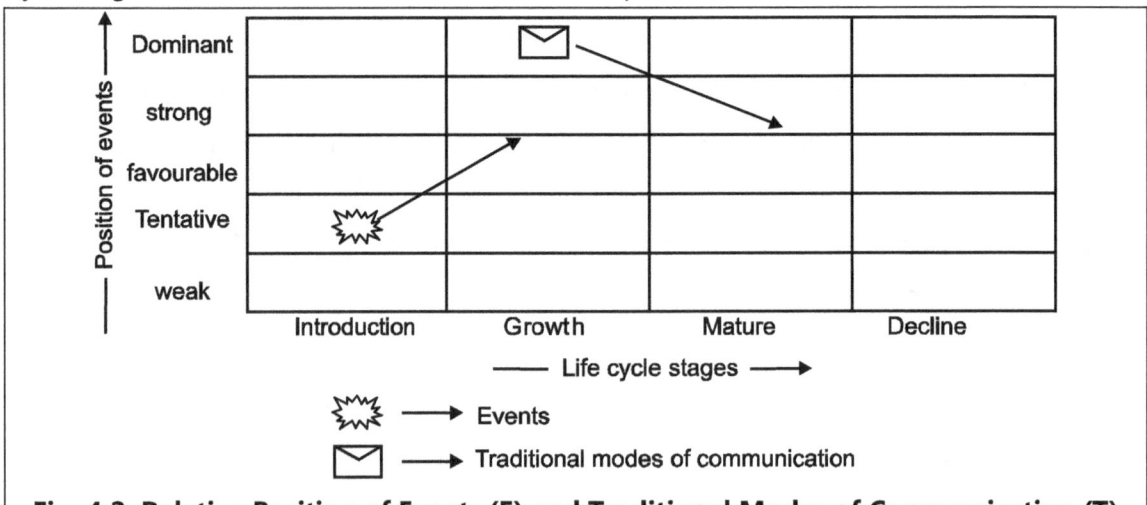

Fig. 4.2: Relative Position of Events (E) and Traditional Modes of Communication (T) with Life Cycle Stages.

Relative position and life cycle stages can be judged on the basis of the characteristics of the industry. The demand and popularity of the various media help determine the life cycle stage of the media as well as their relative positions in relation to other media. This representation clearly indicates the growing importance of events. It clearly shows that –

Traditional ways of most popular modes of marketing communication as denoted in matrix moving from the growth phase into the maturity stage. Their effectiveness is lost due to the cut-throat competition which is leading to undesirable clutter in all kinds of media including the Internet.

An event as a medium is now in a tentative/favourable position, will continue to remain so in the near future, and tends towards becoming stronger. Event organising as an industry is still in the nascent or introductory stage when seen in the light of commercialisation and corporatisation of events as a business proposition. Events as a strategic marketing communications tool would gain significant followers and will bite into a much larger portion of the marketing budget. Some voids still exist though and these are beyond the event organisers and clients' control. But over a period of time, these may also be sorted out.

4.11 IMPLEMENTATION OF MARKETING PLAN

Successful marketing of the event will take into account the event objectives (to raise awareness of a cause) and the target audience (their habits, the media they watch or listen to, hobbies). It should also take into account –

1. **Publicity:** The coverage given to the event by media.

2. **Promotion and Advertising:** Publicity that is paid for in order to have control of the communication message. Promotion and advertising should inform audiences about key details of the event (where it is, when, how much, why is it being held, contact information). Paid promotion is often expensive, so it is worthwhile being creative with options.

3. **Sponsorship:** An excellent way of obtaining resources or help for an event. Not only are in-kind arrangements possible (prizes for a raffle), sponsors can also offer cash, discounted leasing of premises (room hire discount) and networks and contacts to use.

Events help in carrying out certain marketing activities by –

1. **Enabling authentic test marketing.** Events bring the target audience together, thus creating a chance for test marketing of products for genuine feedback. The seller can identify precisely the characteristics that are required.

2. **Enabling focus sales and communication to a captive audience.** In an event, the audience is more or less bound to witness one specific event. In such circumstances, it is good for sellers to give their presentations without any distractions.

3. **Increasing customer traffic in stores.** At times newly opened venues, showrooms, retail outlets, etc. need to draw the attention of their target audience and tempt them to visit again. To increase customer traffic, concepts can be formed for events. Specific events can be conceptualised ranging from retail stores on a small scale to an in-between link connecting an increase in customer traffic with a mega-event.

4. **Enabling sales promotions.** Sales promotion is an important gainer from the benefits that events offer. Just upon entering the hall of any event, a questionnaire is given and with the promise of a lucky draw the visitors are persuaded to fill up the form instantly. The questionnaires generally requests personal information such as age group, marital status and monthly income etc. The lucky draw is just a formality but the firm gets the database, which can be segmented and targeted.

5. **Helping in relationship building and PR activities.** Event marketing campaigns have the ability to form long-lasting relationships with closely targeted market segments. Building relations is not limited to end user customers; most events are also targeted at improving distributor and sales representative relations.

6. **Entrusting and motivating the sales team.** The need for the interaction is not limited to external customers only and end consumers are not always the focal point of the live media exercises. To start a product within the firm, events are used as a platform.

7. **Providing an avenue to affirm presence**. After the reformation of the relationship between the collaborating firms, there is a need to give out the right signals to the world that they are in good shape and ready to bounce back into the market with new energy, to guarantee its investors as well as customers of its strong presence in the minds of its stakeholders and the general public.

8. **Generate immediate sales.** Most events install an exclusive booth and give the permission to make use of the opportunity to merchandise. Events such as annual limited period discount sales or stock clearance sales have a goal to generate instant sales.

9. **Generating instant publicity.** On executing a marketing strategy, an event can be designed to generate instant publicity and benefit all the strategic partners.

10. **Recruit new distributors and sales representatives.** In newer territories, it is seen that in trade fairs or exhibitions, companies are continuously on the lookout for new distributors and sales representatives. This is particularly so when overseas business partners are sought after. The fact that the visitors to the event are real, coupled with the chance to communicate over a period of time, lends credibility to this exercise. Contacts made during these events can create long-term business relationships that are commercially advantageous to all.

4.12 RELATIONSHIP BUILDING

In every aspect of life we are in, whether getting involved in the social activities, building our career path, or socialising with our family and friends, we interact with various types of individuals. Such interaction may occur with familiar people with whom we are in close contact like our family and friends or with new acquaintances. We may also build a connection over a period of time with our work colleagues or members in a club. The fact that we interact with people everyday means we are building a relationship with these individuals as we associate ourselves with them in one or the other way.

Relationship-Building Strategies for Your Business

Successful companies don't just communicate with prospects and customers for special sales. Nowadays, making your firm indispensable is an important key to marketing success. It's a terrific way to add value, improve your brand and position against your competition. Here are seven relationship-building strategies that will assist you in transforming your firm into an important resource and to get customers to think of your company first –

1. Communicate frequently: How often do you connect to customers? Do the bulk of your communications concentrate on product offers and sales? For best results, it's significant to talk often and vary the kinds of messages you send. Instead of a continuous barrage of promotions, add them in useful newsletters or softer-sell messages. The exact frequency you select will depend on your industry and even seasonality, but for many types of businesses, it is possible to combine e-mail, direct mail, phone contact and face-to-face communication to keep prospects moving through your sales cycle.

2. Offer customer rewards: From retail to cruise and travel, customer loyalty or reward programmes work well for many companies. The most effective programmes offer graduated rewards, so the more customers spend, the more they earn. This rewards your best, most profitable clients and cuts down on low-value price switchers-customers who switch from programme to programme to get entry-level rewards; whenever possible offer rewards that will remind the customers of your company and its products or services.

3. Hold special events: The company-sponsored golf outing is back. With a new interest in retaining existing customers, company-sponsored special events are returning to the forefront. Any event that allows you and your employees to communicate with your best customers is a good bet, whether it is spring time golf outing, a summer time pool party or an early fall barbecue. Just select the venue most suitable for your exclusive customers and company.

4. Build two-way communication: When it comes to customer relations, "listening" is as significant as "telling." Use every tool and chance to create communication, including asking for feedback through your website and e-newsletters, sending customer surveys (online or offline) and providing online message boards or blogs. Customers, who know that they're "heard", immediately feel a bond with your firm.

5. Enhance your customer service: Do you have an enthusiastic staff or channel for resolving customer issues quickly and efficiently? How about online customers help? One of the best ways to be of importance and stand out from the competition is to have better customer service. Customers often make choices between parity products and services on the basis of the perceived "customer experience." This is what they expect to get in the way of support from your firm after a sale is closed. Top-flight customer service on all sales will help you build repeat business; create positive word-of-mouth and increase sales from new customers accordingly.

6. Launch multicultural programmes: It may be time to add a multilingual part to your marketing programme. For instance, you might offer a Spanish-language translation of your website or use ethnic print and broadcast media to reach niche markets. People from different cultures and backgrounds will welcome marketing communications in their own languages. Bilingual customer service will also be successful toward helping your firm build relationships with minority groups.

7. Visit the trenches: For several businessmen, especially those selling products and services to other companies, it is important to rise above standard sales calls and off-the-shelf marketing tools so as to build associations with top customers or clients. When was the last time you spent your day with the customer – not your sales staff, but you, the head of your company? There's no better way to really understand the challenges your customers face and the ways you can help meet them is to occasionally be in their shoes. Try it. You'll find it can be a real eye-opener and a great way to strengthen lasting relationships.

Events help in relationship building by –

➢ Giving relationship management a proactive feel. Events held together by more than one company help in not only building up a rapport with the customers, but also help in reducing the cognitive dissonance, which is very common. This type of relationship is very proactive in nature because many studies have proved that reduced cognitive dissonance leads to the repeat purchase of the brand.

➢ Creating a forum for bringing together key corporate influencers, decision-makers and businessmen. The forums provide a platform for presentations and discussions on products and packages with key people.

➢ Creating a forum for career match-making. The forums facilitate a friendly and face-to-face interaction between the professionals looking for career opportunities with recruiters looking to hire the best talent.

4.13 THE DIVERSE MARKETING NEEDS ADDRESSED BY EVENTS

Event products generally include a combination of goods and services, and so provide a challenge for those involved in event marketing. When marketing something purely intangible, there is a large service component. In some respects, it is far more difficult to market something that the customer cannot take home or physically consume. An event, whether it is a one time or an annual event, is highly perishable. Unsold tickets cannot be put out on a rack at a reduced price. Services provided at events, then, are intangible, inseparable, variable, and perishable, presenting a number of marketing challenges, since value for money is generally an issue for the consumer.

We can summarise the diverse marketing needs addressed by events as follows: brand building, focusing on the target market, implementing a marketing plan, marketing research, relationship building, and creating opportunities for better deals with different media, events and economy.

4.13.1 Brand Building

Events can help in brand building by –

1. **Creating awareness about the launch of new brands/products:** A random survey of marketing and other management magazines including newspapers would

disclose the huge number of brand/product launches that take place every month. Thus, there tends to be a clutter of product launches too and these may not necessarily create confusion among the same product group. Thus, the need to attract the target audience, at the time of launch, becomes all the more significant.

2. **Presentation of brand description to highlight the added features of product/service:** Sometimes technological changes or policy changes show the way for manufacturers or service providers to expand their products/brands. To express this through conventional modes of communication to the existing and potential customer base may sometimes be futile or ineffective. Special service camps or exhibitions are the perfect events that give the chance for a two-way interaction and error-free communication.

3. **Helping in rejuvenating brands during the different stages of the product life cycle:** The huge amount of money that is spent during introducing the products gets radically reduced after a while. By the time the product reaches its maturity/decline stage, the need for cutting down the budgets connected to the media campaigns, while simultaneously maintaining the customer base is felt. And events offer the best medium for such a focused approach. It helps in generating feelings of brand loyalty in the products' end user by treating them as royally as possible.

4. **Helping in communicating the repositioning of brands/products:** By organising or connecting to events targeted at a specific target audience, it becomes possible to reposition the exercise to be carried out effectively. In other words, one can also say that events can be designed to help in changing beliefs about companies/products/services.

5. **Associating the brand personality of clients with the personality of target market:** Merchandisers, who themselves cannot arrange for premium events on a big scale, take part as clients to connect the personality of their products and brands with the personality of the customers of the event organisers.

6. **Creating and maintaining brand identity:** When the event is promoted by a celebrity, then the brand gets the identity of it.

7. **Image building:** In addition to the brand identity, when a firm encourages some special events, it creates a bond between the firms, the customer, and the product as well as amongst the participants themselves. With a big audience, the event becomes the natural ground for image building.

Enhancing a brand's equity directly through advertising campaigns and indirectly through promotions such as cause championing or event sponsorship is termed as brand building.

> **Touch-points Are Key to Building a Strong Brand:** Customers experience your brand in a number of ways: products, packaging, price, marketing, sales personnel, etc. Each of these contacts or touch-points shapes the customer's impression of the brand. Some of these touch-points are noticeable, like product performance, and one-on-one customer interactions. Other touch-points, such as the product manual, monthly statements or post-sales support, may be subtler in their brand effects.
>
> Your brand image creates expectations. It defines who you are, how you work, and how you're different from your competitors. Basically, your brand image is a promise that must be kept.
>
> If the brand is a promise you make, then the customer experience is the fulfillment of that promise. The customer experience can't be left to chance. It should be designed and controlled in a way that improves your brand image. It must constantly reinforce the brand promise across every customer touch-point or the value of the brand itself is at risk.

Below are given five easy steps for a company to build a strong brand and an optimised customer experience.

> **1. Identify your reasons-to-believe.**
> **2. Identify customer touch-points.**
> **3. Determine the most influential touch-points.**
> **4. Design the optimal experience.**
> **5. Align the organisation to consistently deliver the optimal experience.**

1. Identify your reasons-to-believe

If your customers do not believe in your brand promise then it is irrelevant. Therefore, your promise should be supported by reasons-to-believe. This will automatically add matter to the promise and define particular expectations for the customer.

For instance, an automobile manufacturer promises potential customers that Car XYZ is an "intelligent choice for serious drivers." What makes it an intelligent choice? Why should the customer believe this promise?

To tackle this question successfully, the manufacturer could outline its promise with two reasons-to-believe... sporty performance and safety. These two reasons basically define "intelligent choice" and clearly establish customer expectations. They also give the company specific direction for designing the customer experience through concrete customer touch-points like vehicle design features, advertising campaigns, dealer sales approaches, and customer service activities.

2. Identify customer touch-points

Each individual step in your business process includes numerous touch-points when the customer comes in contact with your brand. Your final goal is to have each touch-point reinforce and satisfy your marketplace promise.

Walk through your commercial procedures. How do you generate customer demand? How are products sold? How do your customers use your products? How do you give after-sales support?

This complete trace of your marketing, selling, and servicing processes enables you to form an easy touch-point map that defines your customers' experiences with your brand.

3. Determine the most influential touch-points

All touch-points are not created the same. Some will of course play a bigger role in determining your firm's overall customer experience. For instance, if your product is ice cream, taste is normally more significant than package design. Both are touch-points, but each has a different impact on our customers' experiences altogether.

To decide the touch-points driving your customers' overall experience, your company can use an extensive variety of methods ranging from quantitative research to institutional knowledge. The techniques you use will depend on the difficulty of your products, commercial processes, and your existing knowledge base.

4. Design the optimal experience

Once you have finished the above three steps required to build a brand, you should be capable of designing your optimal customer experience.

Here's how: Decide how to communicate each reason-to-believe at each key touch-point. For instance, how can you reinforce sporty performance in product design, at the dealership, and in marketing campaigns?

5. Align the organisation to consistently deliver the optimal experience

A holistic approach to support your company to constantly deliver the optimal experience is important. Identify the people, procedures, and tools that drive each key touch-point.

Look past employees that have direct contact with your customers. The effects of behind-the-scenes employees are less obvious but no less significant. In the same way, the effect of workflow processes and tools on the customer experience may be less spontaneous but important to consistent delivery.

Identify which activities don't adjust to your envisioned customer experience. Decide how to address them so that these parts can be aligned.

The Final Word

Every product or service you bring to market yields a customer experience. Is it the experience you propose? Does that experience satisfy the promise you've made to the marketplace?

By recognising the people, procedures, and tools that drive your customer experience, you can design and control your own, unique, optimised experience. The brand promise you make to the marketplace will be kept everyday across every important customer touch-point, building a strong brand.

4.13.2   Focusing the Target Market

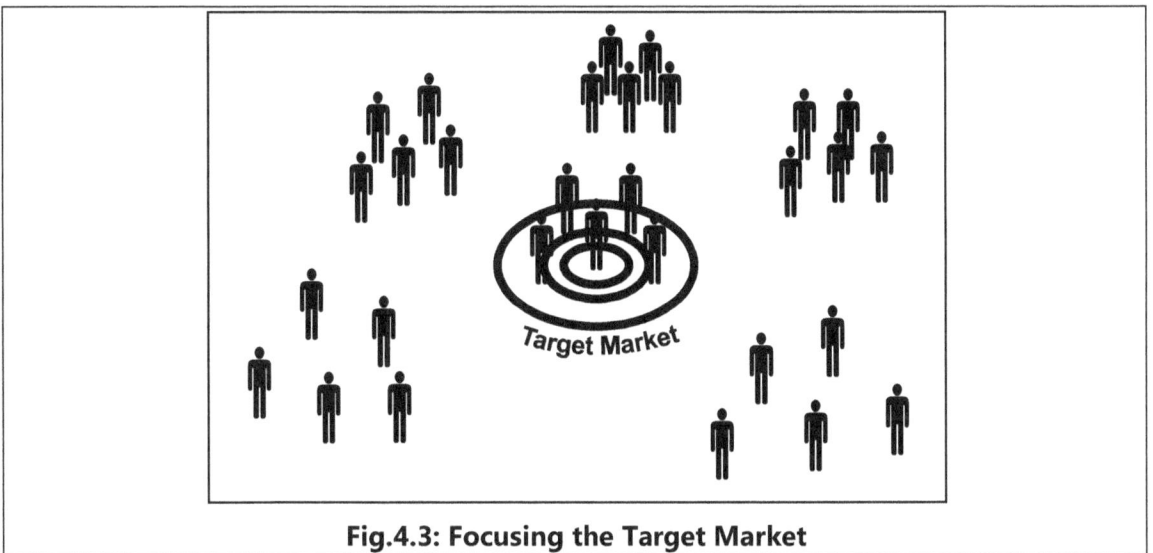

Fig.4.3: Focusing the Target Market

Target Audience: Target audience includes the customer groups who form the focus of events. The actual event design varies with the demographic profile of the target audience as well as the number of targeted audience. It is from these criteria that the event gets its image and budget. Whether the event would be a mega-event or theme parties, which artist would perform or where the event is to be held etc. primarily depend on the target audience. Therefore, starting from the initial conceptualisation to the carrying out of the event the entire process cognizably takes into consideration the characteristics and the behaviour of the target customer groups.

Every marketing activity is essentially customer-based depending on the clients marketing requirements; as discussed earlier, event organisers decide the audience to be targeted. Based on the target audience as a common denominator, the event organiser can canvass for other clients who would like to associate with the event. Thus events can also act as a converging ground for an associate with the event, thus events can also act as a converging ground for a diverse range of corporate with the same target audience, the costing of an event will also definitely vary with both the profile and number of audience being targeted.

Every aspect of the event marketing needs to start with a comprehensive understanding of the target market. In the case of events, the ideal event attendee represents the target market. **People won't buy tickets for an event (or attend a free event) that doesn't hold their interest.** A lack of interest is one of the biggest reasons that events fail. If one wants to pack the event, the best place to start is with a hungry market.

One can find a hungry market by doing a little online research. If it is a new event, target market research needs to be the first planning step. Start by asking, "**What are the target market's wants, needs, and fears as they pertain to the event?**" When asking the question it's really important to take one's ego out of the equation. Focus should be on the market's ego.

Use the Net to Do Free Research

There is a plethora of tools a company can use to research its target market that's topically related to the event. Most of the tools are free. **Pay particular attention to online user content such as comments or reviews.**

Don't Reinvent the Wheel

When it comes to events, there is little need to constantly "reinvent the wheel." If one takes a look at similar and competing events or contact the organiser, then one telephone call could make that event more financially successful or save the heartache. **It's amazing how willing other event organisers are to share information.**

Go Back to Customer List

If it is a recurring event, one should go back to the customer list to find out what people thought of the previous event and what they expect from the next one. The idea is to give people after finding out what they expect from your event.

Build a Profile

Use the target market research to compile a demographic and psychographic profile of the event attendee. The profile represents the ideal prospect and should drive everything what one does with the event website and the event. The profile should also drive the advertising and marketing decisions.

The target market research isn't the most exciting activity, but its importance is paramount. **There is zero benefit in planning or creating an event if people aren't going to attend.** Doing a little homework can save a tonne of money and agony down the road.

Events help in focusing the target market by:

➢ **Helping in avoidance of clutter:** Even though some events do get congested with too many advertisements due to their popularity, events still provide an effective means of being spotted and aid in decongesting the advertising clutter.

➢ **Enabling interactive mode of communication:** Events generically provide an opportunity for buyers and sellers to interact. They also provide a foundation for exchange and sharing of knowledge between professionals.

4.13.3 Creating Opportunities for Better Deals with Different Media

Why does one want to advertise? What is the objective of advertising? What does one want to get through advertising? For example, you want to advertise to create awareness about your event or you want to advertise to get sponsors and clients for your events or you want to advertise to thank your sponsors and clients.

How are you going to promote your event company, your organisers, your sponsors, your clients and your partners, pre-event, at-event and post-event? Before we go any further, let's get an idea of what is media and what is the media vehicle.

Media refers to various means of communications: Broadly speaking there are five categories of media: Print, Electronic, Outdoor, Transit and Miscellaneous media. Print media includes: newspapers, magazines, press releases, tickets, passes, invitations, banners, posters etc. Electronic media includes TV, Radio, Internet, Telephone, electronic signage etc. Outdoor media includes Hoardings, Billboards, and Balloons etc. Transit media includes promotion through cars, cabs, buses, trucks, trains, planes etc. Miscellaneous media includes everything else like events, word of mouth publicity etc.

Media vehicle is a specific medium: For example, if 'Internet' is media, then MySpace, Facebook, Twitter, Google, Yahoo etc. are media vehicles. If 'TV' is a media, then specific TV programmes like 'Coffee with Karan' or 'Dance India Dance' is a media vehicle. Similarly if magazine is a media, then specific magazine say 'Filmfare' or 'Inside-Outside' is a media vehicle.

A single sponsor may find it difficult to network with the different media. The volume of business generated by one sponsoring firm may not be lucrative enough for the particular media to offer substantial room for negotiation whereas professional event organisers are in touch with the media components daily. This enables negotiations by event organisers to be more fruitful than when an individual company negotiates with the media. Negotiations could be in terms of rates offered free in relation with the sponsorship amount. While on TV and radio, free commercial times are bartered by the event organisers, in the print media, advertising space can be bartered. This may not be possible for individual clients.

4.13.4 Events and the Economy

Events and particularly special events are typically regarded as major generators of economic activity and jobs. Over and above the marketing angle, the economic benefit to the region hosting the event is also a positive aspect. Countries like India should be not only investing in information technology but also other communication infrastructure to be ready in this millennium to host similar mega-events. The singular importance of mega-events in driving an economy into growth phase has already been emphasised. And India needs events like these.

One might think that in a tough economy event fund raising is a difficult proposition. However people are much more generous knowing that things are tough and they are often willing to support a worthy cause. Event fund raising can be a challenge. Even in tough economic times one can do quite well by catering to the local area's strengths and by tapping more prominent people in the area.

A festival, either one-time or annual, can provide the kind of economic stimulus required to perk up a lagging economy. The economic objective of the event should be both to circulate cash within your community and bring in cash from outside. Throughout the process, goodwill and community spirit will be generated. A successful and well-planned event stimulates community pride and also it will leave fond memories with visitors, encouraging them to come back again.

In the Annual Special Events Survey, one finds that the Corporate Event Market will be looking up in 2010 and 2011. The mood in the corporate special event community is definitely picking up. It shows growing event rosters, with 18 percent of respondents saying they expect to stage more events in 2010 than they did in 2009, and 35 percent predicting even more event work in 2011. This is a big improvement over last year's study. The corporate events mean business, now more than ever.

4.14 CONCEPT OF AMBUSH MARKETING

What is called in marketing lexicon as parasitic marketing is called as ambush marketing when used with regards to events. Ambush marketing is a word that is used to indicate such marketing activities of a disassociate company through which it tries to borrow the imagery connected to the event. Ambush marketing tries to rob the important benefits from the event and the establishment behind it. Unlike official sponsors who pay important amounts to help support the event, ambush marketers pay nothing.

The "Nothing official about it" campaign by Pepsi when Coca Cola had won the right of being the official drink of the Cricket World Cup' 96 in India is a very live example of ambush marketing. In such cases, there is little the organiser can do, as the ambushers don't use the event's name or logo. Recently, contracts between sponsors and event organiser have included clauses where it is compulsory for the event organiser to assist and support the sponsor in any litigation that can be conducted against such activities. The event firm can barely do anything in this case except try to keep the customer from losing faith in events and preventing their client from separating themselves from the event.

Points to Remember

- A market consists of all the potential customers sharing a particular need – Prof. Philip Kotler.

- In events, there are two distinct types of customers – revenue generating customers and non-revenue generating customers.

- Revenue generating customers are classified primarily into two categories, clients and target audience.

- The clients includes the institutions, corporate houses, media houses like press, TV, radio etc.

- The target audience is the ultimate customer for the event who actually participates in the event.

- Non-revenue generating customers are the indirect customers who mostly are the most active carriers of word-of-mouth policy and do not necessarily generate a monetary gain for the event organisers.

- Revenue is generated from these customers in different forms such as sponsorships, charity and sales of tickets.

- The success of an event depends on the right segmentation and targeting of customers.

- The event organisers should first segment clients and on this basis, proceed to segmentation of target audience.

- The segmentation of the market can be carried out on the basis of the core concept preferences of the clients as well as those of the target audience.

- The target audience can be segmented based on standard demographic, geographic, economic and psychographic traits.

- Some event organisers prefer to focus on a niche area within a chosen market segment. By catering to specific events and restricting their focus of clients and target audience, event organisers can seek to fulfill the needs of a smaller sub-segment within a market segment whose needs are not being well served.

- Once the market segments have been defined, it is imperative that the event organiser selects one or more of these segments to enter, consolidate and grow. That is targeting.

- To establish and communicate the organisers' products through the event to the market is known as positioning.

- The event property also has the characteristics that it belongs to the event organiser and cannot be taken away or stolen by competitors.

- The core benefit offered by any event is the reach with interaction for brand building addressed to a sharply defined and controlled target audience.

- In the event hierarchy, the need family consists of the core need satisfied by using events which is brand building with interaction followed by the event family, which consists of the various categories of events that satisfy the core need.

- The core concept is responsible for giving rise to event categories and delineating the basic differences amongst them.

- Variations in the core concepts distinguish the various categories of events. Events as a marketing tool can be broadly categorised as Competitive Events, Artistic Expressions, Cultural Celebrations, Exhibition Events, Charitable Events, and Special Business Events.

- Competitive events can be divided into various types. These are contests which test sporting skills, artistic talents, knowledge levels or a combination of these or compare participants on the basis of any other parameter as a constraint within a certain set of rules and regulations applicable to all.

- Competitive events are primarily used for visibility and exposure to the brands, prolonged impact, corporate/brand awareness, consolidating the positioning of brands, merchandising and sale of licensed products around the event.

- Creative minds and spirits also equally share the limelight when it comes to competition.

- Music concerts, dance ballets and other stage performances are the most popular forms of artistic expression.

- Get-togethers and celebrations of events that carry mythological, religious significance and/or have traditional values attached by a particular community with homogeneous characteristics.

- Fairs and festivals have their root in religious tradition and rituals basically designed to pass on knowledge to the next generation by the elders.

- Special business events being different and getting noticed for direct commercial gain usually provide equal opportunity for reach and interaction.

- With the entry of multinational brands into India, there has been a sudden spurt in mega-launch activities using innovative ideas.

- Creating and celebrating an event is a sort of investment in brand building.

- Special events with a common objective – to generate sales are expected to attract customer traffic.

- Merchandising events, demonstrations and showings, special sales inducements, film and television-based events, web-based events are the special events.

- Though the categorisation of events as a whole may seem to be comprehensive, they are not exclusive in nature.

- Several variations of the events categories can be created by changing the event design with the help of various factors such as time, risk, budget, location, value, concept, artists and the client.

- Pre-planned events are events that occur or are made to occur on a regular basis and on fixed dates.

- Ad-hoc events can be described as events that come in between fixed events. These are irregular and need to be conceptualised and executed at short notice.

- Risk rated events are sponsored events, partially sponsored events, and ticketed events.

- Budget-based events can be big budget or small budget events that vary relative to the strategic intentions of the stakeholders involved in the event.

- The larger the interaction and reach that is desired, the bigger the budget.

- Events that involve more of interaction with a limited number of audiences are usually small budget events.

- Location-based events are events with a predominantly similar profile for a given location undergo variations based on location essentially due to the demographic changes that occur from place to place.

- Value-based events arise from the value addition that they can provide to their clients.

- Value addition is deemed to be high when the event organisers provide all services right from conceptualisation to carrying out of the event.

- The conceptualisation process is a churning process in which constraints forced by the demands of costing, canvassing, customising and the feasibility of carrying out are accommodated to fit the clients' needs.

- Whether the artist or star performer fits into the concept and is the artist available again depends on the time frame involved in planning of any event.

- The concepts and all other elements of an event will also depend on the type of industry that the client competes in.

- Each event, even within the same category and variation, will differ vastly in the way it is priced.

- The event organisers need to price the event separately for clients and target audience.

- All the three alternatives – whether the event will be fully sponsored, partially sponsored and partially ticketed or fully ticketed, carry different levels of risk.

- From product launches to press conferences, companies create promotional events to help them communicate with clients and potential clients.

- Experience alone can help in identifying the direct relevance of the information to the event pricing.

- We can summarise the diverse marketing needs addressed by events as follows: brand building, focusing the target market, implementation of marketing plan, marketing research, relationship building, and creating opportunities for better deals with different media, events and economy.

- Events can help in brand building by –

  1. Creating awareness about the launch of new brands/products.

  2. Presenting of brand description to highlight the added features of product/service.

  3. Helping in rejuvenating brands during the different stages of the product life cycle.

  4. Helping in communicating the repositioning of brands/products.

  5. Associating the brand personality of clients with the personality of target market.

  6. Creating the brand identity and maintaining it.

  7. Image building.

- Enhancing a brand's equity directly through advertising campaigns and indirectly through promotions such as cause championing or event sponsorship is termed as brand building.

- Target audience is the customer groups who form the focus of events.

- Every aspect of event marketing needs to start with a comprehensive understanding of the target market.

- Successful marketing of the event will take into account the event objectives – to raise awareness of a cause and the target audience – their habits, the media they watch or listen to, hobbies and also publicity, promotion, advertising and sponsorship.

- Events help in carrying out certain marketing activities by –

  1. Enabling authentic test marketing.

  2. Enabling focused sales and communication to a captive audience.

  3. Increasing customer traffic in stores.

  4. Enabling sales promotions.

  5. Helping in relationship building and PR activities.

  6. Entrusting and motivating the sales team.

  7. Providing an avenue to affirm presence.

  8. Generate immediate sales.

  9. Generating instant publicity.

  10. Recruiting new distributors and sales representatives.

- Interacting with people everyday means that we are building a relationship with these individuals as we associate ourselves with them in one or the other way.

- Seven relationship-building strategies : 1.Communicate frequently. 2. Offer customer rewards. 3. Hold special events. 4. Build two-way communication. 5. Enhance your customer service. 6. Launch multicultural programmes. 7. Visit the trenches.

- Events help in relationship building by –

  1. Giving relationship management a proactive feel.

  2. Creating a forum for bringing together key corporate influencers, decision-makers and businessmen.

  3. Creating a forum for career match-making.

- There are five categories of media: Print, Electronic, Outdoor, Transit and Miscellaneous media.

- A single sponsor may find it difficult to network with the different media. Professional event organisers are in touch with the media components daily. This enables negotiations by event organisers to be more fruitful than when an individual company negotiates with the media.

- Events and particularly special events are typically regarded as major generators of economic activity and jobs.

- According to Annual Special Events Survey, the Corporate Event Market will be looking up in 2010 and 2011.

Questions for Discussion

1. What do you understand about the concept of market and describe the distinct types of customers for events?

2. What is segmentation and targeting of the market for events?

3. Explain in detail the positioning and branding in events with the concept of event property.

4. Describe the characteristics of the different categories of events.

5. What are the important factors in pricing of events?

6. Explain the relative importance of events as a marketing communication tool.

7. What are the diverse marketing needs addressed by events and explain any two of them in brief.

8. How do the events help in building the brand?

9. What is the target audience and how do you find them?

   (ii) In what manner do events help in marketing activity?

   (iii) What is relationship building? What strategies you will have for building relationships?

10. How do events help in building relationships?

Chapter 5...

Strategies of Event Management

Contents ...

Learning Objectives ...

After going through this chapter, you will be able to gain an insight into the following

- To get acquainted with the strategic approaches to event management.
- To understand critical success factor analysis.
- To study different strategic alternatives.
- To learn to do critical evaluation of events.

5.1 STRATEGIC APPROACH

Strategy refers to an elaborate and systematic plan of action designed to achieve a particular goal.

Johnson and Scholes, Corporate Strategists, define strategy as: "Strategy is the ***direction*** and ***scope*** of an organisation over the ***long-term***, which achieves ***advantage*** for the organisation through its configuration of ***resources*** within a challenging ***environment***, to meet the needs of ***markets*** and to fulfill ***stakeholder*** expectations".

Strategy is the means by which objectives are pursued and obtained over time. One, who learns this, will enable him to apply strategic thinking to their lives, through understanding strategy and putting it into practice.

Strategy at Different Levels of a Business

Strategies exist at different levels in any organisation – ranging from the overall business through to individuals working in it.

1. **Corporate Strategy:** It is concerned with the overall purpose and scope of the business to meet stakeholder expectations. This is an important level as it is deeply influenced by investors in the company and acts to guide strategic decision-making throughout the business. Corporate strategy is frequently mentioned clearly in a "mission statement".

2. **Business Unit Strategy:** Is concerned more with how a company competes successfully in a specific market. It concerns strategic decisions about choice of products, meeting requirements of customers, gaining advantage over competitors, exploiting or creating new opportunities etc.

3. **Operational Strategy:** Is concerned with how each part of the business is organised to deliver the corporate and business-unit level strategic direction. Operational strategy thus concentrates on issues of resources, processes, individuals etc.

In other words, strategy is about

1. Where the business is trying to get to in the long-term (**direction**).

2. Which markets a business should compete in and what type of activities are involved in such markets (**markets; scope**).

3. How the business can perform better than the competition in those markets (**advantage**).

4. What are the needed resources (skills, assets, finance, relationships, technical competence, facilities) required in order to be able to compete (**resources**).

5. What effect external, environmental factors have on the businesses' ability to compete (**environment**)?

6. What the values and expectations of those who have power in and around the company are (**stakeholders**).

This signifies nothing but the strategic approach towards business.

1. Strategy is the criterion which determines what an opportunity and strength is, as well as gives the guidelines to identify potential weaknesses and threats.

2. Phenomena and events in the real world do not always fit a linear model. Hence the most reliable means of dissecting a situation into its constituent parts and reassembling them in the desired pattern is not a step-by-step methodology such as systems analysis. Rather, it is that ultimate nonlinear thinking tool, the human brain.

3. True strategic thinking thus contrasts sharply with conventional mechanical systems approach based on linear thinking. But it also contrasts with the approach that stakes everything on intuition, reaching conclusions without any real breakdown or analysis.

4. No matter how difficult or unmatched, unprecedented the problem, a breakthrough to the best possible solution can come only from a combination of rational analysis, based on the real nature of things, and imaginative reintegration of all the different items into a new pattern, using nonlinear brainpower.

5. This is always the most effective approach to devising strategies for dealing successfully with challenges and opportunities, in the market arena as on a battlefield. The aim of a strategy is ensuring long-run returns.

6. A strategy as such which does not result in immediate tangible benefits. It lends an aura of comprehension to the task at hand, ensuring that the big picture is not lost. The nitty-gritty of actual decision-making and tactics in executing an event can take its basic root from a strategy.

Now, if the competitive advantage distinguishes business competitive advantage, there would be no need for strategy, for the sole purpose of strategic planning is to enable the company to gain a sustainable edge over its competitors as efficiently as possible. A distinction is made here between relative strength and absolute strength, reserving the term strategy for actions aimed at directly altering the strength of the enterprise relative to that of its competitors. One will find a great difference in the terms relative and absolute strength if the degree of urgency is observed. Internal weaknesses can be tolerated for time being. But deterioration of a company's position relative to its competitors may endanger the very existence of the enterprise. In effect, the company's profitability will be allowed to be controlled by its competitors and a situation in which sound management of the enterprise will no longer be possible.

Another very important reason is that strategic planning requires a specific type of thinking. When one is striving to achieve or maintain a position of relative superiority over a dangerous and deceitful competitor, the mind functions very differently from the way it does when the object is to make internal improvements with reference to some absolute model. It is the difference between going into battle and going on a diet.

Strategic approach is creating a planned approach, focused on agreed challenges and opportunities and identifying responsibilities for making things happen. The significant benefits of a strategic approach are –

1. Long term
2. Identifying linkages
3. Adding value
4. Enabling different interests to work together
5. Creating synergy
6. Developing a common vision and objectives
7. Agreement on priorities; open and shared by the community and agencies
8. Tackling the most important things first
9. Addressing of problems and barriers at an early stage
10. Avoiding wasting resources on inappropriate developments
11. Providing a powerful tool for working with agencies and achieving funding

Strategic decisions should invariably be preceded by the critical success factor (CFS) analysis. The critical success factor analysis for the events industry, for example, SMART events could be as discussed and given in the next section.

Strategic planning and management are more than a set of managerial tools. They constitute a mind-set, an approach to looking at the changes in the internal and external environment that confront the event manager.

Using planning and management tools strategically, then, involves essentially a way of thinking, a mental framework or approach, as well as a set of analytic tools.

For strategic management to be effectively used the event manager must develop a strategic mentality or outlook. The problem for the consultant is how to help the manager acquire that mentality.

The Strategic Approach

The strategic approach consists of four main elements:

1. First, the strategic approach is oriented toward the future. It recognises that the environment will change. It is a long-range orientation, one that tries to anticipate events rather than simply react as they occur. The approach leads the manager to ask what his goals are, what he will need to do to get where he wants, and how to develop strategies and the means to get there, and finally, how to manage those strategies to achieve the events goals and objectives. It is recognised that the future cannot be controlled, but the argument can be made that by anticipating the future, event organisations can help to shape and modify the impact of environmental change.

2. Second, the strategic approach has an external emphasis. It takes into account several components of the external environment, including technology, politics, economics and the social dimension. Strategic thinking recognises that each of these can either constrain or facilitate an organisation as it seeks to implement policy. Politics will determine the policies that are to be implemented, economics will determine the organisation's level of resources, and social factors might well determine who the organisation's beneficiaries will be. In particular, strategic thinking recognises and emphatically takes into account politics and the exercise of political authority. Managers are not free to do anything they decide. Managers must be sensitive to the needs and respond to demands of constituents over whom they have little or no control. Among those constituents, political actors are perhaps the most important.

3. Third, the strategic approach concentrates on assuring a good fit between the environment and the events, mission and objectives, strategies, structures, and resources and attempts to anticipate what will be required to assure continued fit.

Under conditions of rapid political, economic and social change, strategies can quickly become outmoded or no longer serve useful purposes; or the resources traditionally required by the organisation to produce its goods and services may suddenly become unavailable. The strategic approach recognises that to maintain a close fit with the environment, the different elements of the organisation will need to be continuously re-assessed and modified as the environment evolves.

4. Finally, the strategic approach is a process. It is continuous and recognises the need to be open to changing goals and activities in light of shifting circumstances within the environment. It is a process that requires monitoring and review mechanisms capable of feeding information to managers continuously.

5. Strategic management or planning are not one-shot approaches, they are ongoing. When all are taken together, these attitudes and behaviours are really a way of approaching or thinking about how to manage or how to implement policy change. Strategic management (or planning) is not something that can be applied only once and then forgotten about or ignored. In that sense it is more than a tool; it is a mental framework.

An event manager who takes the strategic approach to event management can be assured of success. Time and effort must be spent by event organisations on determining their long-term attitude towards the staging of events. It is important to establish an event strategy to make clear the direction in which an event is heading. Bidding to stage a single event should never be done in isolation.

1. The strategy should present a concise strategic overview of event-hosting aspirations.

2. The strategy is not an application to receive funds for specific events.

3. Dates for bidding for and staging events are often established many years in advance.

Every successful marketing event begins with a vision of the result, a goal to meet and a strategy to get there. Without these three things, events are left to struggle and never become as big or as profitable as possible. Your strategy is the "How" to your vision's "Why" and your objective's "What". Whether you charge an admission fee or not, your attendees also invest in your event with their time. To get the best outcomes from your marketing event, your event strategy has to have these five elements in place.

An Event That Sells

An event that sells begins with the name. You want to have a catchy title for your event that attracts the target audience and compel them to come to your event. State the advantages that your attendees will get, what is it that they will come away with? If you have formed your vision, you already know what that is, so it should be simple to add in a strong benefit statement into your event name. Weave the benefit statements throughout your marketing and concentrate on what your event will do for your attendees, their lives and their companies.

Content That Rocks

Your event content should be "New, Now, Next". Your attendees clamour for new data and insights, strategies that they can execute now and tools they can continue using next week, month and year. Particularly if you use your workshop or seminar to sell your services on the backend, your event should have a lot of content. If your content is light and your sales pitch is heavy, you will lose your audience. People do business with individuals they know and trust. To be the first person to do business with the people you like, you have to give them valuable content that makes them happy they invested their time and money with you.

A Venue That Works

Every workshop, seminar, and event is different and you can use many different venues for your event. The key is to use the type of venue that is good for your event. Whether that is a hotel, conference centre, library, community centre or another venue depends on your vision. If your vision comprises of a simple, educational background, a conference centre or a university would work. If your target market is of women who are high spenders and who are used to comfort and an expensive lifestyle, a community centre or school cafeteria will definitely not work. Make your venue work for your vision, your target market and your event.

Revenue Streams That Explode Your Profits

Charging admission for your events is a clear revenue stream, but it is not the revenue stream that makes you rich. Create a package of products and services with a special workshop price to sell in the back room. You can also create information of the products from the event. Record yourself and create a course that can be studied at home to sell on your website. You can use a one hour section as a lead generator to capture the traffic on your website.

Event Elements That Add Value

When you know what benefits your attendees are looking for, you can add elements that strengthen the benefits and increase the value of the overall experience. If one of the benefits to come to your event is to make relations with likeminded people, ensure you build in opportunities for them to do just that. Add a welcome reception so your attendees can get to understand each other in an informal setting, breaking the ice a little. For a one day workshop, add a roundtable lunch, where each table has a subject to talk about. Individuals interested in that topic can sit at that table and have a conversation with fellow attendees interested in that subject.

You will be successful during planning your marketing if you have your goal as target, event strategy in place and your vision in mind. Your strategy and its components will guide you to plan an event that will take your business to the next level. Connect with your customers like never before, turn them into raving fans and create a profit avalanche. It all occurs when you host your own live event.

5.2 CRITICAL SUCCESS FACTOR ANALYSIS

Critical Success Factors (CSFs) have been used significantly to present or identify a few key factors that organisations should focus on to be successful. As a definition, critical success factors refer to "the limited number of areas in which satisfactory results will ensure successful competitive performance for the individual, department, or organisation".

Identifying CSFs is important as it allows firms to focus their efforts on building their capabilities to meet the CSFs, or even allow firms to decide if they have the capability to build the requirements necessary to meet Critical Success Factors (CSFs).

CSFs are the essential areas of activity that must be performed well if one is to achieve the mission, objectives or goals for a business or project.

By identifying the Critical Success Factors, one can create a common point of reference to help one direct and measure the success of a business, event or project.

As a common point of reference, CSFs help everyone in the team to know exactly what's most important. And this helps people perform their own work in the right context and so pull together towards the same overall aims.

The idea of CSFs was first presented by D. Ronald Daniel in the 1960s. It was then built on and popularised a decade later by John F. Rockart, of MIT's Sloan School of Management, and has since been used extensively to help businesses implement their strategies and projects.

Rockart defined CSFs as

"The limited number of areas in which results, if they are satisfactory, will ensure successful competitive performance for the organisation. They are the few key areas where things must go right for the business to flourish. If results in these areas are not adequate, the organisation's efforts for the period will be less than desired."

He also concluded that CSFs are "areas of activity that should receive constant and careful attention from management."

Critical Success Factors are strongly related to the mission and strategic goals of a business or event or project. Whereas the mission and goals focus on the aims and what is to be achieved, Critical Success Factors focus on the most important areas and get to the very heart of both what is to be achieved and how one will achieve it. Critical Success Factors (CSF's) are the critical factors or activities required for ensuring the success of a business. The term was initially used in the world of data analysis and business analysis. These have been used significantly to present or identify a few key factors that organisations should focus on to be successful.

Being practical, there are potentially a variety of definitions and uses of Critical Success Factors. Before one starts the journey looking at CSFs, it is important to realise that the specific factors relevant for, will vary from business to business and industry to industry. The key to using CSFs effectively is to ensure that your definition of a factor of your organisation's activity which is central to its future will always apply.

Therefore, success in determining the CSFs for the organisation is to determine what is central to its future and achievement of that future.

How are they important to the particular business?

Identifying CSFs is important as it allows firms to focus their efforts on building their capabilities to meet the CSFs, or even allow firms to decide if they have the capability to build the requirements necessary to meet Critical Success Factors (CSFs).

Main Aspects of CSFs

CSFs are tailored to a firm's or manager's particular situation as different situations (for example, industry, division, individual) lead to different critical success factors. Rockart and Bullen presented five key sources of CSFs – the industry, competitive strategy and industry position, environmental factors, temporal factors, and managerial position (if considered from an individual's point of view). Each of these factors is explained in greater detail below.

Critical Success Factor Analysis: Using the Tool-Summary Steps

In reality, identifying CSFs is a very iterative process. The mission, strategic goals and CSFs are intrinsically linked and each will be refined as they are developed.

Here are the summary steps that, used iteratively, will help to identify the CSFs for an event or project –

1. **Step One:** Establish the event or project's mission and strategic goals.

2. **Step Two:** For each strategic goal, ask "what area of business or project activity is essential to achieve this goal?" The answers to the question are the candidate CSFs.

Rockart's CSF types as a Checklist

To make certain one considers all kinds of possible critical service factors, one can use Rockart's CSF types as a checklist.

Industry: These factors result from certain industry features. These are the things that the company must do to remain competitive.

Environmental: These factors result from macro-environmental influences on an organisation. Things like the business climate, the economy, competitors, and technological advancements are incorporated in this group.

Strategic: These factors result from the specific competitive strategy selected by the organisation. The manner in which the firm chooses to place and market themselves, whether they are high volume low cost or low volume high cost producers, etc.

Temporal: These factors result from the company's internal forces. Specific barriers, challenges, directions, and influences will decide these critical success factors.

---

3. **Step Three:** Evaluating the list of candidate CSFs to find the absolute essential elements for achieving success – these are the Critical Success Factors. As one identifies and evaluates candidate CSFs, one may uncover some new strategic objectives or more detailed objectives. So one may need to define your mission, objectives and CSFs iteratively.

4. **Step Four:** Identify how to monitor and measure each of the CSFs.

5. **Step Five:** Communicate the CSFs along with the other important elements of the event business or project's strategy.

6. **Step Six:** Monitoring and re-evaluating the CSFs to ensure one is moving towards the aims. Indeed, whilst CSFs are sometimes less tangible than measurable goals, it is useful to identify as specifically as possible how you can measure or monitor each one.

Critical Success Factors are the areas of a business, event or project that are absolutely essential to its success. By identifying and communicating these CSFs, you can help ensure your event or project is well-focused and avoids wasting effort and resources on less important areas. By making CSFs explicit, and communicating them with everyone involved, you can help keep the event and project on track towards common aims and goals.

Critical success factor analysis is a technique to identify those areas in which a business must outperform the competition in order to succeed. Strategic decisions should invariably be preceded by the critical success factor (CFS) analysis.

Limitations

A key limitation of the critical success factors technique is the qualitative aspect to recognising them. As they are developed from the industry to the firm and maybe to the individual level, there is an important degree of inconsistency that could result from the qualitative input needed. Thus, there could be important differences in what different people think critical success factors in industries and organisations to be, necessitating substantial effort and discussion in determining them.

Critical success factors are used by organisations to focus on numerous factors that help in defining its success. They assist the organisation and its employees to know the important areas in which to invest their resources and time. Ideally, these critical success factors are observable in terms of the effect on the organisation to allow it to guide and indicate its achievement of them.

Critical success factors can be used in both the organisation and the individual levels. Their identification is mainly qualitative and can result in varying opinions in identifying them. However, it is an approach that should be followed as it gives value in giving due focus to a limited set of factors, which are considered to be the most important for an organisation or individual.

5.3　STRATEGIC ALTERNATIVES ARISING FROM ENVIRONMENTAL ANALYSIS

An analysis of the internal and external environment is a significant part of the strategic planning process. Environmental factors internal to the company generally can be classified as strengths (S) or weaknesses (W), and those external to the company can be classified as opportunities (O) or threats (T). Such an analysis of the strategic environment is called as a SWOT analysis.

The SWOT analysis gives information that is useful in matching the company's resources and capabilities to the competitive environment in which it works. As such, it is involved in formulating strategies and selection.

Internal External	Strength	Weaknesses
Opportunities	**Maintenance Strategy** Utilising the company's strengths to take maximise advantage of opportunity.	**Developmental Strategy** Maximise opportunities by minimising weaknesses.
Threats	**Pre-emptive Strategy** Maximising strengths and their usage to overcome threats.	**Survival Strategy** Minimise both weaknesses and threats by considering options such as joint ventures, retrenchment, liquidation etc.

Fig. 5.1: SWOT-based Strategy Matrix

5.3.1   Maintenance Strategy

Arising from circumstances of strength and favourable opportunities, the maintenance strategy gives reasons to perform activities that make best use of available advantages. This is the perfect position to be in. Beyond this, every activity concentrates on maintaining the winning edge and the lead over competitors. The event firm here can afford to be aggressive understanding very well that it has the related strengths to back its claim on the opportunity.

5.3.2   Developmental Strategy

To take advantage of potential opportunities while not having enough strength but still win by using tactical retreats were unrelated yet not given up. It needs passive and defensive strategy, which attracts related opportunities in such a way as to hide inherent weaknesses. A similarity here could be from the game of test cricket where a side that understands victory is impossible also understands that it can ward off a defeat by trying for a draw. This can be called a development strategy where one attempts to make the most of the opportunity by not giving into weaknesses.

5.3.3   Pre-emptive Strategy

This strategy is generally used by established market leaders on new entrants on their turf. Potential threats are cut off by using complete power of the firm's strengths. This is a very powerful and aggressive strategy as it needs foresight to completely understand the threats looming on the horizon. Choosing which one to deal with needs careful study as some points of strength could get eroded if used needlessly.

5.3.4   Survival Strategy

This strategy is used to guarantee that the firm is alive for a battle on another day when it will have the strength to grab its share of opportunities in the market. This strategy gives permit to take decisions like leasing one's soul to the devil if only with an aim to get it later. Simply, it enables one to make drastic decisions even with a harsh environment.

5.4   STRATEGIC ALTERNATIVES ARISING FROM COMPETITIVE ANALYSIS

A mapping of event concepts can be used as a changeable component together with decisions on facing competition, further to the strategy from the environmental analysis, which can bring about more detailed and in-depth strategic options.

Event Concepts

		Use Existing	Create New
Compete		**Sustenance strategy.** Manage critical success factors more effectively.	**Rebuttal strategy.** Respond to new initiatives by competition with a similar move.
Avoid Head-on Conflict		**Accomplishment strategy.** Relative superiority. Exploit competitor's weakness.	**Venture strategy.** Maximise user benefits by using path breaking trend-setting initiatives to take a lead versus competition by being first in the market.

Fig. 5.2: Concepts vs. Competition Matrix

5.4.1   Sustenance Strategy

This is a strategy that is to be used when there is no option but to take on the opponent with the existing weapon of event concepts that may be old or still existing but almost to the end of its lifecycle. It becomes important that the event firm manage its resources and advantages with regards to critical service factors that have been identified with greater effectiveness. Successful ideas need to be improved and revamped to meet customer expectations in the face of competitive offerings.

5.4.2   Rebuttal Strategy

If the competition forces new concepts first then the rebuttal strategy must be used. In this, the event firm can launch its own new ideas of a similar vein and regain its leading position by forcefully promoting the same as a better option. This way the market's education about the new idea is left to the competition and an advantage gained is that market response to particular new concepts is visualised. The disadvantage lies in namely because the first mover's advantage is lost.

5.4.3   Accomplishment Strategy

This strategy is possible when an existing idea is doing better than any of the competitors' equal offering. This strategy, thus, basically says those "stick to the winning concepts and exploit the fact that competition cannot provide the same quality concept and thus wants to avoid a head-on conflict by itself". The danger here is that competition may use any of the other strategic options available to a challenger to combat the situation.

5.4.4   Venture Strategy

This strategy foresees making use of the first mover advantage by creating new ideas prior to the competition thereby creating niche markets. This may even involve a re-definition of market segmentation. By maximising user benefits and creating path-breaking, trend-setting ideas the event firm places itself to take a lead in relation to competition by being first in the market. This is a double-edged strategy in that failure is as overwhelming and devastating as the advantages of a successful launch.

5.5   STRATEGIC ALTERNATIVES ARISING FROM DEFINED OBJECTIVES

1. What are the basic reasons for any event to happen?
2. For whom or at whom – the customers or clients, the event is targeted?
3. How to deal with existing clients?
4. What to offer clients at different stages of a relationship on the basis of the objectives?

Event Concepts

	Existing	New
Existing	Retain client	Increase productivity of clients
New	Increase productivity of concepts	Market development

Fig. 5.3: Client vs. Concept Fit Matrix

The matrix of clients versus event concepts provides options that event customisation have an offer in terms of concepts and their market. The basic strategic alternatives revolve around whether the objective is to retain customers or market development. These objectives further lead to the strategic options of achieving them either through customisation or new concept development. By offering new concepts to existing customers, a strategy of increasing business from existing clients can be discerned. Similarly by offering an existing event to a new client, a strategy of increasing productivity of the event concept can be followed.

5.6   PREP MODEL

Alternative strategies to catch the attention of and retain clients regarding the competitors' activities are presented in this model developed by **Gaur and Saggere**.

This framework has its roots in the fact that event as a business proposition for corporatisation is comparatively nascent in nature. Thus, the idea of strategic perspective to growth through and together with the customers is a major growth plan. This section deals with the strategic alternatives available by playing off goals relating to market development against growth in competition.

The above matrix vocalises the choices before the event firm when it comes to a trade-off between clients and competition with regards to assigning priorities in decision–making.

Clients		
	Existing	**New**
Competition **Existing**	Enrichment – Strategy	Predatorily Strategy
New	Retaliatory Strategy	Proactive Strategy

Fig. 5.4: PREP Matrix

If the development of new clients from existing competitors is the need of the situation then the event firm would be accepting the predatorial market development strategy. This is basically an offensive, though focused strategy wherein clients of other event firms are targeted.

5.7   RISKS VERSUS RETURN MATRIX

The business is always associated with the risks and an understanding of those risks associated with the business is involved in the strategic planning. Depending on the type of events, the risks and returns that mount up are shown in the below given matrix, considering the two most important risk factors, as well as the degree to which it can affect the events company – planning lead time and type of finance.

Events based on the lead time can be divided into pre-planned events, that is, events carried out after thorough planning with enough time for taking conscious decisions and ad hoc events, that is, those that are taken up on the spur of the moment. Events based on the type of finance can be divided into fully sponsored, fully ticketed or partially ticketed and sponsored. As we can see from the matrix, each decision carries with it an element of risk, the gradations of which can vary from zero risk to very high risk.

Time		
	Pre-planned	**Ad hoc**
Fully Sponsored	**Zero Risk** Assured Returns	**Low Risk** Assured Returns (can change extra since chances of failure are high.)
Partially Sponsored and Ticketed	**Medium Risk** Assured Returns to cover costs + chances of loss are low.	**High Risk** Assured Returns to cover costs but lower chances of profits.
Fully Ticketed	**High Risk** Chances of high profits with equal chances of losses.	**Very High Risk** Very less time to ensure reach. Chances of failure and loss are high.

Fig. 5.5: Risk vs. Return Matrix

5.8   FORMS OF REVENUE GENERATION

Every event generates revenue and depending on the type of event, the revenue comes in different forms like sponsorships, charitable contributions, corporate philanthropy, and charitable contributions by corporate, ticket sales etc. While organising an event, the event organisers should have their clear-cut objectives in mind about the revenues to be generated. Mainly revenue comes from the sponsors in most of the events. In commercial, leisure and organisational events, different types of sponsorships and ticket sales are the ones used for revenue generation, while in charity events all the forms of revenue generation may be used. Normally personal events do not generate any revenue.

5.8.1 Developing a Media – Rights Strategy

For many events especially sports events the money from broadcasters for the right to show television footage of their events has become a very significant income stream. For this reason many will have longstanding arrangements with broadcasters which cover events over several iterations.

This is not always the case and many event organisers will have the discretion and indeed be expected to make local arrangements for delivery to television audience. This is, of course, vital to rights-holders who want to drive interest in their events and to sponsors whose investment is thereby multiplied.

5.8.2 Sponsorship

Sponsorship is another area where global rights may already have been sold by rights-holders but it is likely that event organisers will have the opportunity to raise money from their domestic brands.

5.8.3 Ticketing and Hospitality

Some of the most important decisions an event organiser will take will be around ticket sales. Priced too low and vital money will be lost, priced too high and the take-up among the local community will fall short leading to embarrassingly empty venues.

Having set prices and created packages to suit all expected visitors, event organisers will need to consider whether to sell tickets directly or share the load with a ticketing agency. And, once tickets are sold they will need to look at the secondary market as that is where the hottest tickets may end up.

5.8.4 Licensing and Merchandising

Beyond the ticket itself, for example in sports events, many fans value the chance to demonstrate their allegiance during the event. Flags, scarves, hats, shirts and even horns build atmosphere in the stadium and provide a significant income stream.

Fans will often purchase other programmes, souvenirs and other memorabilia of their experience and event branded goods can be a way for a local community to show their support for an event in a practical way.

5.9   THE BASIC EVALUATION PROCESS

Evaluation is an activity that seeks to understand and measure the extent to which an event has succeeded in achieving its purpose. The purpose of an event will differ with respect to the category and variation of event. However, to provide reach and interaction would be a generic purpose that events satisfy.

(a)   The extent to which an event has succeeded in achieving its objectives and purpose is to be understood and measured in the basic process of evaluation.

(b)   The purpose of an event will differ with respect to the type and category of the event, except the generic purpose of providing reach and interaction.

(c)   The concept of evaluation has emerged from the critical examination digging out what went wrong

(e)   It is essential that every event should have the pre-defined objectives and they should be properly communicated to and understood by the event organisers. The total evaluation would be pointless if there are not clearly defined objectives and purpose and the event has been organised.

This evaluation process involves three basic steps as follows –

(a) Establishing tangible objectives and incorporating sensitivity in evaluation.

(b) Measuring the performance before, during and after the event.

(c) Correcting deviations from plans.

A more constructive focus and aim for evaluation is to make recommendations about how an event might be improved to achieve its predefined objectives and purpose more effectively.

The fundamental reason why event evaluation is carried out is to navigate the event so as to ensure that the event objectives are achieved in total. And since deviations may occur during any stage in the event designing phase, it is important that measurement is carried out at all possible stages.

The Basic Event Evaluation Process

In events, the basic evaluation process involves three steps –

1.   Establishing tangible objectives and incorporating sensitivity in evaluation

2.   Measuring the performance before, during and

3.   After the event correcting deviations from plans

These steps are discussed below.

5.9.1   Establishing Tangible Objectives / Incorporating Sensitivity In Evaluation

As discussed in Chapter 2, setting objectives for an event is really crucial as it is entirely depending on the briefing from the client to create and customise the event concept. It is very easy to set the objectives but really tough task to establish tangible objectives. An event may be conceptualised to achieve different objectives from different audience. Therefore, the first step is to identify the target audience and then the client's objective from that target audience, that is, what is expected from the target audience of the event. This makes the evaluation measurement proceedings concrete in practical.

As the costs of production and organising events are high and also increasing exponentially, the clients or the companies definitely want to check the effectiveness of their events as to whether their purpose is fulfilled and their money is being spent on the event prudently.

The evaluation should be objective and should take into consideration the nature of the concept and the process of execution of the event in their entirety. There is a scope for error and misjudgement even if evolution is however professional. This is because it takes a creative and sensitive mine to spot wrong questions or situations where asking questions might be a wrong method and observation might be more appropriate. One of the ways of nurturing and encouraging this sensitivity is to place evaluation within the context of a team approach all the way from conceptualisation to carrying out of the event. Adding sensitivity to the evaluation process is very important.

Setting objectives for an event is easier said than done. It is more difficult to set standards and declaring an event successful after it meets them. To provide tangibility to the problem, the best approach is to begin with definition of the target audience for whom the event has been organised. In the case of commercial events, the audience could be end users who use the company's products. An event might be conceptualised to achieve different things for different audiences. Once the audience has been defined, the next step is to identify and put on paper what each of the audience is expected to think, feel and do having been to the event, that is, it did not think, feel or do beforehand. This adds an element of tangibility to the evaluation and measurement proceedings.

The number of mega-events has increased dramatically in the past few years and the costs of organising events have also increased exponentially. The costs of production in major events can be enormous and therefore, in the near future one can expect companies to start asking questions about the effectiveness of their events to see whether their money is being spent prudently.

Creativity is derived from the Greek word 'enthous' which literally translates into 'god within'. Setting out to evaluate such an effort that is considered to be the work of gods themselves demands a certain amount of sensitivity during evaluation. Objective evaluation should also take into consideration the nature of the concept and the process of execution of the event in their entirety. However professional the evaluation, there is scope for error and misjudgement if sensitivity is not adhered to. This is because it takes a creative and sensitive mind to spot wrong questions or situations where asking questions might be the wrong method and observation might be more appropriate. One of the ways of nurturing and encouraging this sensitivity is to place evaluation within the context of a team approach all the way from conceptualisation to carrying out of the event.

From experience it is known that people involved in an event are more open minded and less committed to any particular course of action before the event occurs. Yet another understanding is that if things are shown to be wrong after a decision has been taken, the majority of people involved in the decision-making process may try to wash their hands of the fault. Thus, adding sensitivity to the evaluation process is very important.

5.9.2 Measuring Performance

Performance measurement should be ideally done against the set objectives and on a positive and forward looking basis. Though measuring performance perfectly is not always possible practically, but the occurrence and may be avoided by appropriate actions.

The measurement of performance against the objectives should ideally be done on a forward looking basis so that deviations may be detected in advance of their occurrence and avoided by appropriate actions. Concept research is used to anticipate the viability of a concept during the conceptualisation process. Formative and objective evaluations are carried out during the customisation phase of an event. Summative evaluation can be carried out to measure performance during the event.

1. Concept Research

During the conceptualisation process, concept research is used to anticipate the inability of a concept. At the conceptualisation stage, a commissioning of audience research is appropriate to be adopted in the event to make a sound decision between various available options. It essentially involves presenting the various options to a representative sample of the target audience in a story form and inviting their reactions about. This process provides enough grounds for understanding the pros and cons of the various available alternatives. As it deals with the plans to be implemented, this method called as concept research is speculative in nature.

2. Formative Evaluation

Evaluation at this stage focuses on things that are actually happening. After the conceptualisation team makes an attempt to customise and implement an agreed strategy, steps can be taken to evaluate the success with which customisation is proceeding.

These evaluations are aimed at shaping the form of the final event. Mock-up displays and presentations of the event are used to carry out research to check whether they are achieving the desired reactions from the audience.

These evaluations are conducted among small sample representative of the target audience in an open-ended and qualitative fashion since the main emphasis is on discovering how the concept might be better represented.

The outcome of these formative evaluations lead to a discussion among the team in which proposals for rectifying any weak points in the communications can be put forward. A point, which should be safeguarded against whilst using this technique, is to interpret consumer reactions with considerable sensitivity to stimulate the creative process further and also to ensure that good ideas are not killed simply because they were not properly presented in mock-up form.

3. Objective Evaluation

This is the stage when approval from the client is sought before starting the execution related activities of an event. The evaluation team has to provide the objective evidence that has been collected which justifies the proposed concept solutions. The team also provides reassurance on how and why the particular event will work among its intended audience. Since taking the client into confidence requires certain amount of objectivity and professionalism, this technique is called objective evaluation.

4. Summative Evaluation

The evaluation team should be concerned with measuring the impact of the event on the audience, finding out the extent to which the established aims and objectives have been met or whether the event can be improved in any manner and how. The main purpose of the summative evaluation after the event is to provide the team with the opportunity of the learning from their mistakes, so as to avoid making similar mistakes in the future.

5.9.3 Correcting Deviations

To ensure whether the event objectives are achieved in total is the prime motto of the evaluating the event. And since deviations may occur during any stage in the event designing phase, it is important that measurement is carried out at all possible stages.

5.9.4 Critical Evaluation Points

Events can be evaluated based on the critical success factors listed below; from both the clients' and event organiser's viewpoints.

While evaluating events critically, evaluation should be based on the clients, points of view as well as organisers point of view.

When a team evaluates an event, they should check on these following points from the client's point of view so as to get the effectiveness of the event.

1. Immediate and tangible benefits achieved like actual sales, number of enquiries generated, number of prospects to be, as well as leads generated during the event.

2. Cost effectiveness of the event.

3. Intangible and long-term benefits achieved like brand image, goodwill, product launching and attendance of targeted audience and the acceptance, etc.

Following points are to be considered while evaluating an event from an organiser's point of view –

1. The effectiveness of the event – whether the client has achieved the set objectives or not.

2. Cost effectiveness of the event.

3. Cost-benefit analysis.

4. Time management.

5. Percentage of the turnout of the targeted audience, etc.

Points to Remember

- Strategic approach is creating a planned approach, focused on agreed challenges and opportunities and identifying responsibilities for making things happen.

- An event manager who takes the strategic approach to event management can be assured of success. Time and effort must be spent by event organisations on determining their long-term attitude towards the staging of events. It is important to establish an event strategy to make clear the direction in which an event is heading.

- Critical Success Factors are the essential areas of activity that must be performed well if one is to achieve the mission, objectives or goals for an event, business or project.

- Critical Success Factors are strongly related to the mission and strategic goals of a business or event or project. Whereas the mission and goals focus on the aims and what is to be achieved, Critical Success Factors focus on the most important areas and get to the very heart of both what is to be achieved and how one will achieve it.

- Critical success factor analysis is a technique to identify those areas in which a business must outperform the competition in order to succeed. Strategic decisions should invariably be preceded by the critical success factor (CFS) analysis.

- An analysis of the internal and external environment is an important part of the strategic planning process. Environmental factors internal to the firm usually can be classified as strengths (S) or weaknesses (W), and those external to the firm can be classified as opportunities (O) or threats (T). Such an analysis of the strategic environment is referred to as a SWOT analysis.

- The strategic alternatives that arise from an analysis of the environment include Maintenance Strategy, Developmental Strategy, Pre-emptive and Survival Strategy.

- Strategic Alternatives arising from Competitive Analysis include Sustenance, Rebuttal, Accomplishment and Venture Strategy.

- Alternative strategies to attract and retain clients with respect to the competitors' activities are presented in the PREP model developed by Gaur and Saggere.

- It deals with the strategic options available by playing off objectives relating to market development against growth in competition.

- Every event generates revenue and depending on the type of event, the revenue comes in different forms like sponsorships, charitable contributions, corporate philanthropy, and charitable contributions by corporate, ticket sales etc.

- Evaluation is an activity that seeks to understand and measure the extent to which an event has succeeded in achieving its purpose. The purpose of an event will differ with respect to the category and variation of event.

- In events, the basic evaluation process involves three steps:

  1. Establishing tangible objectives and incorporating sensitivity in evaluation

  2. Measuring the performance before, during and

  3. After the event correcting deviations from plans

Questions for Discussion

1. What is Strategic Approach with respect to Event Management?

2. Explain Critical Factor Analysis.

3. Explain in brief any two Strategic Alternatives.

4. Explain the risk versus return matrix in Event Management.

5. Describe basic evaluation process critically.

APPENDICES

APPENDIX A : TIME MANAGEMENT IN EVENTS

Become observant of yourself and others. The first step to becoming a good time manager is to observe the ways you are currently spending your time and write it down. Take notice of where your time goes and where and with whom you spend it. Once you are aware of where your time goes, it will be much easier to determine what you should do differently. The second step is to make better choices. The idea of trying something new can be intimidating, but if you don't change what you're doing then you'll keep getting exactly what you're already getting.

Learn To Say "No"

Saying "no" is very hard for some people, but it has tremendous rewards. Ask yourself "what" is the wisest and best use of my time right now ? " If any given opportunity does not meet that criterion, say "no" to that opportunity.

Plan 10 Minutes Every Day

Taking less than 1 per cent of your day to plan the other 99 per cent will yield much more than the cost of 10 minutes. The many benefits of a written plan include the ability to recover faster from interruptions, to control events instead of being controlled by them, and to save the time lost transitioning between tasks. You don't save time by skipping the planning process, you lose it.

Prioritise

The Pareto Principle, or the 80/20 rule as it is sometimes called, was discovered by the Italian economist Vilfredo Pareto back in the early 1900s. Pareto suggested that 80 per cent of the results we get come from 20 per cent of the things we do. So the question is, what activities create 80 per cent of the results?

Psychologists say there are only two forms of human motivation

To move toward gain or to prevent pain. "Gain" activities include whatever moves you toward your goals. Anything that pertains to how you want to be remembered fits into this category. "Prevent pain" activities include all responsibilities that would eventually find you if you neglected them. Activities that move us toward gain produce 80 per cent of the results in our lives while the ones that prevent pain produce 20 per cent. Great time managers have gain activities as a consistent part of their day.

Undercommit and Overdeliver

This is one of the greatest productivity secrets of all time. So often we tend to do the opposite. This one skill alone can reduce tremendous amounts of stress in your life and significantly strengthen your relationships.

Use One Time Management System

There is no greater cause of stress then not delivering on a commitment. Whether its your mortgage or rent commitment or a commitment you make to a customer or fellow employee, not following through or under delivering causes us a great deal of stress. Have a system that brings your commitments to you without all the worry. Don't let elusive floating scraps of paper be your only reminder of commitments. Gel them all in one system.

Find a Mentor or a Coach

Even Michael Jordan needed a coach to achieve his best. Each of us needs a teacher who cheers, us on and teaches us the skills we need to be successful. Find someone who can mentor you and coach you along the path to reaching your goals, if you can't find an all round coach its OK to have more than one. Have a coach for each area you would like to improve.

Get Organised

Documentation is one thing. Documentation retrieval is another. On average you lose an hour a day looking for things. If you want more time, spend less of it looking for what you need. Remember a cluttered desk, car or home is a cluttered mind. The reason we leave things lying around instead of filing or putting them away is because we don't want to forget them. Investing in a planning device or learning how to better use the planning device you already have to help you put things away and not lose track of them is time and money well invested.

If You Can't do it Today Don't Look at it Today

Instead of creating only one "to-do" list, you should have one for each and every day of the year. Day planners, Palm Pilots Outlook and the like give you the ability to schedule activities and projects but few people take advantage of this simple function. Think of the power of this one skill. Now, if you think of something you can't do until next Wednesday, you can put it on next Wednesday's "to-do" list and forget about it. If you consult your plan everyday, that task will come back to you all by itself. If clients ask you to call them back in 3 months, you no longer have to beat yourself up trying to remember. You can let your planning device remember for you. "Future to-do lists" as I call them are the key to goal achievement, effective delegation, project management and making sure the commitments you make don't fall through the cracks.

Turn "To Do's" into Appointments

What is higher in priority than a task that has been prioritised as an "A" on a "to do" list ? The answer is an appointment on your calendar. We defend appointments while we tend to put off tasks. Think of the difference in commitment between having exercise on your "to-do" list and having an appointment on your calendar to meet with a personal trainer. To take your time management skills to the next level take your "A"s off your "to-do" list and put them on your appointment schedule.

Get Motivated

Everyone is motivated differently. Find what motivates you and use it. When you're in a positive mood you can get more done; so use positive material to help you get there. Experts say that more than 87 per cent of what you hear each day is negative. If this is true, you'd better have a way of reducing its effect. Make sure you are getting what you need to stay positive and motivated.

Computer Efficiency

The Speed of your typing and your ability to navigate the computer affect your ability to be productive in a big way. More and more of our time each day is spent on the computer. Make time for computer skills development by either learning from someone skilled, taking a computer class, or just purchasing magazines and iiterature that will give you tips and advice.

You may have heard that time is the one commodity none of us can increase. But that's not exactly true. You can have more time and accomplish more in the time that you have when you make positive changes according to these principles.

Remember, it's your life. So make the most of it!

APPENDIX B : STAGING AN EVENT

This section gives an outline of the issues of staging. By studying the material you should be able to

- ➢ Understand the place of staging in event management.
- ➢ Describe the elements of staging.
- ➢ Apply the tools of staging.
- ➢ Understand the importance of stage safety.

Introduction

No matter what happens with the event planning, risk management or marketing, the event ultimately must be staged. That is, all the entertainment, sound system, lights, food etc. must be put together successfully so that the event itself works for the attendees. The staging of the event is pulling together all these elements. It involves planning what goes on at the event site and co-ordinating it all on the day of the event. You need to

1. Understand what will go on at the event.
2. Work out what'is needed so it can happen successfully.
3. Find all the necessary goods and services.
4. Co-ordinate it all so that it seamlessly fit together.

Looking at each of these steps for a Wine and Food festival

1. There will be wine and food and there may also be music or theatre entertainment, sports competition and children's rides.
2. Each of these elements needs support - or resources. These include sound system, security, power and water, covered stalls, a ticket booth, storage and waste removal.
3. Once all this is listed it must be found - or sourced. This includes finding the right suppliers and advertising for stall space.
4. Finally the pieces of the jigsaw has to form the complete picture. The supplies have to arrive on time, the entertainers have to start and finish on the right stage.

This section will look at the ways of doing all of this successfully. It is divided into three sections.

1. The elements of staging - each of the important elements are discussed with some handy hints.

2.   Tools of staging - techniques and forms that make staging easier to manage and tell everyone what is happening.
3.   Stage safety.

ELEMENTS

Facts

A large part of staging is the co-ordination so that the audience is surrounded by the theme of the event. First you need to create the theme, find the specialists and put the whole show together. Often the work results in a production that is over in a few hours. It is the one area of event management that is obvious to the attendees.

Any mistake is magnified by the fact that the audience win see it all. Therefore, you must have it planned to the finest detail. Just as in the event project management section, you break up the staging into its component elements and then reassemble them for the event. These elements are

Sound

You will almost certainly need to use a sound system at an event. You need to know some of the terms they use if you are to work with them efficiently.

The basic checklist for sound would be

1.   Do you really need it and if so how big will you need? This will depend on many factors, such as room size, number of attendees, indoor/outdoor, noise from audience, noise from other activities, acoustics of the area, budget etc.
2.   Access for sound equipment, i.e. entrances, pathways and locations.
3.   Room for equipment - including the storage of the containers.
4.   Correct electricity outlets and amount of power and generators.
5.   Compatibility with other staging equipment.
6.   Safety issues - such as cabling, weather, speaker volume and placement.
7.   Backup in case of emergencies.

Lights

Lights can enhance the event and they may be necessary as a safety measure as well. The basic checklist for lights would be

1.   What will the lights primarily be used for?
2.   Using existing lighting and their compatibility with the supplier's lights.
3.   Positioning of lights.
4.   Enhancing the theme of the event.
5.   Access and storage of equipment.
6.   Qualified personnel.
7.   Safety including securing light support towers or rigging and their use for safety such as illuminating steps and hazards.

Audio Visual

If the event requires a lot of technical production, it may be wise to employ an audio visual company. The audio visual company will often take over all aspects of the technical side of the event. This is because the technical equipment needs to be compatible with all the other equipment used in the event.

Fireworks and Special Effects

This aspect of staging requires highly trained, and often licensed specialists. You need to specify exactly what you want them to do. You should use their advice — in particular if they see any aspect of your our event that they feel is unsafe. As the special effects will need to be timed they will need to liaise with the other staging elements.

Food and Beverage

Catering at an event can range from simple tea and biscuits to a candle silver service under the stars. Fortunately most professional catering companies have a guideline to their service and offer hints on how to put your event together on their web sites. Catering can be part of the theme - such as a medieval feast - or it can be just a support service to the event. Either way there are strict regulations that you as the event manager need to know. In particular the responsible service of alcohol is important.

The regulations governing this aspect of events vary from state to state and you are strongly to go to you relevant Liquor Licensing board before you plan the event.

Decorations and Props

There always seems to be plenty of help to dress up an event. Decoration and props can be found in all sorts of areas from schools to farms. They should be consistent with the theme of the event. The props should be checked for safety as they are often only temporary structures.

Stage Managers and Other Staff

There is an increasing tendency to use stage managers. It should be remembered that the event stage is very different from the theatre stage and the stage managers should be briefed as to their role and responsibilities. Other personnel such as waiters, bar staff and roadies can to the event theme as well as do their job. It is well to remember that all staff should be briefed about the event theme.

The Stage

Stages can be professionally built structures or just the back of trucks or a few wooden pallets. You need to ask what the stage is for before you consider hiring it. Remember that the stage will have to accommodate more than just the performers. The sound and lights can take up a lot of room.

Steps and Questions

Choose an event and list what is happening at the event.

What are the support goods and services needed to make it all work on the day ? Can you group some of these together so they are done by one company?

Tools and Facts

The two main tools of staging are the stage plan and the schedule.

1.   Stage Plan : It is a map of the staging area. As the stage at an event may be the whole site the stage plan may be based on the site map or it may be a number of areas within the site. The aim of the stage plan is to show the staging support where everything is happening. If it is not clearly drawn then it fails in its purpose.

2. Schedule : It is a list of what is happening and when. If it is a short show with lots of action, the schedule may be detailed and have everything timed to the second. It will be used by all the staging support staff as well as the performers. It should not be confused with the event programme which is the event from the perspective of the audience or attendees. The programme is the result or visible part of the schedule. The schedule can be worked out from the programme. For example, if the programme shows that the fire works will start at 9 pm , the schedule will list the time for setup, show and pack tip. Not everyone working on the event will need to see the whole schedule. A smaller more specific schedule will be worked out for them. These are often called run sheets. For example, the entertainers will not, need to know all the information about the sound schedule for all stages. They only need to know when they rehearse, perform and leave. So they are given a runs sheet for their stage specifically.

Steps and Questions

Sketch out a stage plan for the next event you organise.

Using it as the basic plan, draw the positions of the lights, sound speakers, props and other staging elements. For the complex event, consider using a number of transparencies. Each transparency can be used for each element and superimposed on the basic plan.

Create a production schedule for your next event. Who wit] be using it? How will you reach it to everybody in time? Is it better to give the performers, for example, a part or the entire schedule?

Safety

Where all the actions take place unexpectedly, is the area where accidents occur. Often it is in the dark and, when there is action, it is fast and unexpected. For this reason, safety in the staging area is a priority for you. You must put together a checklist for safety and this must include training the stage staff in safety issues. Often it is easy to ask volunteers to help out in this area; however be aware as it is a specialised field. For example, do you know how hot stage lights are?

Activities

Create a safety checklist for each staging element including such issues as checking equipment on arrival, storage, licensing and ensuring that there are no remaining safety issues that are a result of a combination of the staging elements?

Conclusion

When your audience arrives at an event, they will spend most of their time looking at the area of the staging. Everything that happens there will be noticed. It must be planned and tile various staging elements brought together successfully. It is only by breaking the staging into its components and using the right tools summarised in this section that the complexity of staging an event can be managed.

APPENDIX C : SITE INSPECTION CHECKLIST CRITERIA
(Especially for Residents)

Amenities
1. Ability to display banner in prominent location.
2. Limousines for VIP's.
3. Upgrades to suites available.
4. Concierge on VIP floors.
5. Room delivery for entire group upon request.
6. In room television service for special announcements.
7. Personal letter from venue manager delivered to room.
8. Complimentary parking for staff of VIPs.
9. Complimentary coffee in lobby.
10. Complimentary office service for staff such as photocopying.

Capacity
1. Fire Marshall approved capacity of venue for seating.
2. Capacity of venue for parking.
3. Capacity for exposition booths.
4. Capacity for truck and vehicle marshalling.
5. Capacity for prevent function such as reception.
6. Capacity for other functions.
7. Capacity for public areas of venue such as lobbies.
8. Size and number of men and women's rest rooms.

Catering
1. Full service venue specific Catering Operation.
2. Twenty-four hours room service.
3. Variety of food outlets.
4. Concession capability.
5. Creative tasteful food presentation.

Equipment
1. Amount of rope and stanchions available.
2. Height width and colours available for inventory of pipe and drape.
3. Height width and skirting colour available for platforms for staging.
4. Regulation for use and lift availability for arrival work.
5. Adequate number of tables, chairs and stair and other equipment.

Financial
1. Complimentary room ratio.
2. Guarantee policy.
3. Daily review of folio.
4. Complimentary reception or other service to incurs
5. Function room complimentary rental policy.

Location Proximity
1. Location of venue from nearest airport.
2. Distance to nearest train facility.
3. Distance to nearest fire rescue facility.
4. Distance to shopping area.
5. Distance to recreational activities.

Medical First Aid
1. Number of staff trained in CPR, Heimlich man ever and other first aid.
2. Designated first aid area.
3. Ambulance service.

Registration
1. Sufficient well-trained personnel for check in.
2. Ability to provide express check in for VIPs.
3. Ability to distribute event materials at check in.
4. Ability to display group event name on badges or buttons to promote recognition.
5. Effective directory or other signs for easy recognition.

Site Inspection Checklist Criteria Regulation
1. Designation of a civil defence rescue team to be used in emergencies.
2. Pre-existing prohibitive substance regulations.
3. Other regulations that impede your ability to do business.
4. Fire code requirement with regard to material composition for scenery and other decoration.
5. Local fire officials requirements for permission to use open flame or pyrotechnic devices.
6. Requirement regarding the use of gasoline powered motors.
7. Policy regarding live trained animals.

Safety and Security
1. Exterior and interior walkways are well lit.
2. Venue has full time security team.
3. Communication system in elevators is in working order.
4. Venue has positive relationship with law enforcement agencies.
5. Venue has positive relationship with private security agencies.
6. Fire sprinklers controlled per zone or building wide. Individual zone can be shut off with a fire Marshall in attendance for a brief effect such as pyrotechnics.
7. Alarm systems initially silent or it immediately announces a fire emergency.
8. Condition of all floors including the dance floors.

Utilities
1. Electrical power capacity.
2. Power distribution.
3. Working on-site reserve generator for use in the event of a power failure.
4. Responsible person for operation of electrical apparatus.

5.   Sources for water.
6.   Alternative water sources in case of disruption of service.
7.   Separate billing for electricity or water.

Weight

1.   Pounds per square foot for which venue is rated.
2.   Elevator weight capacity.
3.   Stress weight for items that are suspended such as lighting scenic projection and audio devices.

APPENDIX D : CORPORATE SPONSORSHIP FOR PROMOTIONAL EVENTS AND PROGRAMMES

(a)   Introduction
(b)   What is Corporate Sponsorship?
(c)   Issues to Consider
(d)   What are Corporate Sponsors looking for?
(e)   Researching Prospective Sponsors
(f)   The Sponsorship Proposal
(g)   Closing the Deal
(h)   Nurturing the Relationship
(i)   Conclusion

Introduction

Corporate sponsorship can be a great way to fund health promotion events and programmes that you otherwise would not be able to run. But, it can also be along and time consuming process if done without considering all of the issues or proper research. It can even harm your image if you are not strategic about the corporations that you partner with. Corporate sponsorship as a means of fundraising explains the difference between corporate sponsorship and corporate giving, the issues that should be considered before soliciting sponsors are what corporate sponsors are looking for from a relationship with you. The chapter will also discuss the research process, the important elements of a sponsorship proposal, issues to consider in closing the deal and how to nurture your new corporate relationship.

What is Corporate Sponsorship?

In order to be successful at securing corporate sponsors, you must make sure that it is sponsorship that you are actually requesting. Corporate sponsorship and corporate giving are often used interchangeably but are actually two completely separate acts; the money comes from separate sources, you will deal with separate departments and the goals, objectives and the proposal will all be different.

Corporate giving (or corporate donation) is a philanthropic activity. A corporation will donate money or products and the only acknowledgement they will expect is a tax receipt and a thank you.

Corporate sponsorship, on the other hand, is a business relationship. Corporations look for marketing and community relations opportunities in exchange for money, products or services, and they corporate recognition for their involvement.

There are generally three types of Corporate Sponsorship
1. Event Marketing (sponsorship of a specific event)
2. Partner Sponsorship (a long-term partnership with an organisation or programme)
3. Cause Related Marketing (corporate sponsor promotes a specific cause through the. purchase of their product or service).

Issues to Consider

There are many issues that organisations should consider before leaping into the world of corporate sponsorship. There are many concerns about partnering with corporations and it is important to consider all of the implications corporate sponsorship could have on your clients, volunteers, donors and board members. You will probably want to create a corporate sponsorship policy to guide you. This policy could include a statement of principle, screening criteria for sponsors and an administrative process. There is also an enormous amount of work involved in the research and soliciting and maintaining of corporate sponsorship relationships and it is important for you to have the time and energy to be able to fulfill your promises to the sponsors.

Ask yourself the following questions before you decide to solicit corporate sponsors
1. What are the benefits for our organisation?
2. What risks will there be ?
3. Will associating our organisation with certain corporations affect our credibility ?
4. Is corporate sponsorship appropriate for the nature of the event or programme ?
5. Do we have the resources to be able to effectively support the process of securing sponsors ?
6. Do we have liability insurance that would cover us in the event of a problem ?
7. Are there any philosophical or ethical issues that we should consider ? Are there any guidelines or policies that we should put in place ?
8. What type of screening process will we have ? .

What are Corporate Sponsors Looking for ?

Remember that this is a marketing opportunity for corporations and that you need to have something offer them in return. Not only do they want to increase the awareness of their brand or product but they also want to enhance their image. When deciding to sponsor your event or programme, corporations will ask themselves "What's in it for   us ?"

➢ Will sponsoring this event or programme increase our sales ?
➢ Is there a way for our employees to get involved ?
➢ Is there an opportunity for business to business marketing (e.g. a reception) ?
➢ is there a target audience and product fit ?
➢ Is there a solid PR campaign in place ?
➢ Do we have flexibility ?
➢ Are there complimentary tickets or items available ?

> ➤ How much do we have to do ? (Sponsors want to be able to just show up and' have no additional responsibilities)
> ➤ Does this organization have a good reputation with other sponsors ?
> ➤ Is this a once off or is it annual? (Most sponsors like to build long-term relationships)
> ➤ What risks are involved in sponsoring this event or programme ?
> ➤ Are we being offered industry exclusivity so that we have a competitive edge ?

Researching Prospective Sponsors

The amount and depth of the research that you will need to do will vary depending on how much money you are requesting and the size and types of corporations you plan on soliciting. If you are soliciting sponsors for an expensive nation-wide programme, you will have considerably more research to do than if you are soliciting sponsors for an inexpensive local awareness event. The first step is to develop a list of prospective sponsors.

Think about the nature of your event or programme and consider the following

> ➤ Who is going to be attending the event or be involved in the programme ?
> ➤ What is the age of these participants ?
> ➤ Which gender is more involved ?
> ➤ What is the geographic location of the event or programmme ?
> ➤ What are the ethnic and economic backgrounds of the participants ?
> ➤ What does this group of people do, buy, read, and watch ?
> ➤ What are their interests ?

Consider which corporations might have the same target market as your event or programme. For example, if you are planning a health fair in a rural community for seniors, you would not solicit corporations. But if you were organising a basketball tournament for teenage boys and girls in an urban setting, there would be excellent corporations to include on your solicitation list.

The second step is to qualify your prospective sponsors. You need to determine if the corporation you are considering has the financial capabilities to engage in sponsorship at all or at the level you are interested in. You can do this by contacting organisations such as the Chamber of Commerce etc. It is also important to confirm that the marketing plan of the potential sponsor is a "good fit" with your event or programme. Review the sponsor's past marketing efforts, by reviewing their annual report and studying their advertisements, to see if there is a match. Also, talk to marketing 'executives to determine if your event or programme would be of interest to them -

The last part of your research it to determine the appropriate person to send your proposal to and how long it will take for them to review and consider your proposal.

The Sponsorship Proposal

The sponsorship proposal must convince a potential sponsor that your event or programme is going to meet their business needs. It needs to be visually appealing and easy to comprehend. Mail your proposal to the individual that you have already confirmed as being the appropriate contact. Follow up with that individual every two days from the date of receipt. Be persistent but very pleasant.

Your sponsorship proposal should include the following
- ➤ A description of the organisation that is holding the event or programme.
- ➤ A description of previous events or similar programmes.
- ➤ An overview of the event or programme for which sponsorship is being solicited.
- ➤ A description of who will be attending the event or be involved in the programme, how many and their demographics.
- ➤ Quotes/testimonials from past sponsors and participants from previous events.
- ➤ An explanation for the prospective sponsor of how they will benefit from becoming a sponsor.
- ➤ A detailed media plan for your event or programme.
- ➤ An explanation of sponsorship opportunities (what's in it for them). For example, where their logo and name will be seen and how big will their logo and name will be (on posters, tickets, banners, brochures, booklets, invitations etc.), if there will be verbal recognition at the event, on television spots or at a press conference, opportunities for on-site sampling
- ➤ A list-of what the sponsor will be required to provide (either financially or with products) as well as items such as their logo, banners, signs, booths, staff members.
- ➤ A separate page of contact information so that the corporation can easily find the appropriate person to get in touch with if they are interested in pursuing the relationship.

Conclusion

Corporate sponsorship can be a valuable source of funding for health promotion events and other programmes provided it is done correctly. This means taking the time and resources to first understand how sponsorship will fit with the objectives and policies of your organisation and your event or programme. And secondly, spending the time, energy and resources to do the necessary research, to write a professional proposal and to make sure that you deliver on every promise you have made. If you are new to the sponsorship world, consider starting small. Solicit one sponsor for a local event and then work your way up. Be professional and remember that You are entering a business relationship, which may be a different way of thinking.

APPENDIX E : SELECTING, CONTRACTING AND MANAGING PERFORMERS

By studying this section you will be able to
1. Understand the importance of the performer to the success of the event.
2. Negotiate with performers, their agents or managers.
3. Manage the performers at the event to maximum value.

Introduction

Many of the aspects of managing an event are invisible to the attendees. The performers or artists on the other hand, are the very visible part of the event. No matter what the food, toilets, transport facilities are like, a radiant performance can make the event. It can leave a memory that will never fade with time. Although the artist may only be performing for a few minutes, the event manager has to do all in their power to make sure that those few minutes are brilliant. Hiring performers is not like hiring other suppliers. Their product is often intangible - and for that reason can be the most powerful part of the event. Think back over the events you have attended - was it the toilets or layout that impressed you - or was it the performance.

For this reason, it is a high risk area and therefore needs careful planning. This section outlines the process of hiring performers and the knowledge necessary to get the most from your artists. It is divided into

1.   Selecting performers
2.   Negotiating and contracting
3.   Managing the artists

The information can be applied to any kind of performance. In a way VIPs, guest speakers and politicians are performers and the process equally applies to them.

Selection

(A) Facts

The first question to ask is what are the performers for? Is their primary purpose

1.   To attract a new audience to the event
2.   To satisfy the existing audience
3.   To attract an audience to a future event - such as using them at the launch of a festival or for the inaugural event so that more people will come next year.

If their primary purpose is to attract a new audience to the event then they must be promotable. It is no good having the greatest juggler if no one knows his name. Then he will be incapable of assisting the promotion.

This is the most common mistake of new events. Performers will often welcome any opportunity for self promotion and this should be used to help promote the event. Unless the performers can be used for promotion, their main purpose is to entertain the already existing audience.

There are secondary reasons for using performers such as

1.   **Crowd Control :** clowns can diffuse a potential problem such as long queues, they can assist in moving the attendees to together areas of the event.
2.   **Distraction :** The performers can be used to take the attention away from an area while it is being set up. They can entertain the children so the adults can relax.
3.   Just to give a **general buzz** to the event. They can make dead areas in the event exciting.

Who will you get to give that thrill to an event? A juggler, a judge or a belly dancer or a comedian will depend on the type and style of event, your target market, your sponsors, budget and the 'fit' with the staging and other performers. It will also depend on their availability, talent, price, their sponsors and whether they are easy to deal with.

Assuming you have done your research and know what type of performers will suit the event, the next step is to find them. This can be done through various theatrical or music agencies. A web search, looking a similar event, attending all kinds of events, advertising and auditioning, the phone book, asking suppliers and asking other performers are all good methods of sourcing your performers.

It is wise to get an idea of the performers from a recent performance so that you have experience of their latest skills. You can ask for them to send you a video or photos of their latest performance. Note that these can be expensive items and the job must be worth it from the performer's point of view. Often artists have groups or a collective of friends that do the festival circuit. They can also advise you on other aspects of your event. Although you may only organise a few events per year, the performers may attend over 100 and they have a very good idea. of what would work.

For your next event, make a list of what performers you would like. Estimate their potential to help promote your event. Use the internet to find ideas festivals and performers.

NEGOTIATING AND CONTRACTING

Facts

The basis of all good negotiation is knowledge - knowing what is important to the other party, what they can vary, what is absolutely fixed and what is left unsaid. Hence the best advantage in negotiating a fee with performers is to know exactly how their fees is decided. A performer may have to pay all kinds of commissions such as a 10% agent's fee and a 20% or more manager's fee. Also the fee will have to pay for special clothes, transport, training and rehearsals. On the subject of rehearsals, you should be sure if a rehearsal is necessary and make it clear to the performers when negotiating.

Other costs that may be hidden to you are

1. **Increase in insurance** because of the nature of the performers.
2. **Extra security :** If the performers are famous or infamous you may attract a bigger crowd then you first thought.
3. **Copyright fees :** There are a variety of copyrights that you must be aware of in particular IPRS Music performances and broadcast copyright etc.
4. **Clash of sponsors :** The performers may have a sponsor that is incompatible with the event sponsor.

You should know the way the performers are paid - or the fee structure. It can be a combination of

1. **Fixed Fee :** Just a lump sum.
2. **Variable Fee :** This could be based on the number of people attending.
3. **Guarantee :** Plus a variable fee.

You may be able to reduce the fee by offering accommodation, transport or free tickets. The fee to by paid including the advance and the remainder after the event - must be negotiated and put in the agreement. There may be a request for a cancellation fee.

It is an important to understand that when performers get a job, they may have to turn down other work. Booking (hiring) a performer means that they can not accept other work even if it is far more lucrative.

For this reason you may have to pay the full fee if you cancel a performance. If you have a small event, it is wise to understand how performing at your event will benefit the artist and use this knowledge when negotiating.

When hiring a performer, there may be three different people that you have to deal with

1. The performer.
2. His agent who is concerned with the live performance and generally negotiates the deal with you. They tend to regard the work of the artist as just a series of paid performances.
3. His Manager who is concerned with the career of the artist and how your event will benefit the ongoing work of the artist.

You should establish who has these responsibilities. If you are negotiating with the performer when it is his agent who decides the fee and other conditions; then you may be wasting year time.

The performer contract is a vital document for your event. It is the deal in a written form, hopefully, as unambiguous as possible. Even a simple one page letter with what you are getting and how much you are paying for it is better than leaving the arrangement unrecorded.

If you would like to use the performers to promote the event then it is wise to discuss this early in the negotiation. Do they have photos, video, web page, CDs or gimmicks that can be used to assist in the event promotion. Do they have other performances where they can promote your event ?

Steps and Questions

Examine the next event and, list the ideal performers for it. What would they like to achieve by performing at the event? List the aspects that you think can be negotiated with them.

What are your `non-negotiable' points?

MANAGING

Facts

When dealing with artists, it is well to remember that they are dedicated to their art form. Whether it is mime, public speaking, music or dance, they want to give the best performance. It is often advantageous to regard the artists as partners in creating a successful event rather than employees or subcontractors. Your job is to try to create the right environment so that the artist can thrill the audience. This is not to say you are at their mercy.

However an understanding of their background and art form can be conducive to a good performance. For example, if you are organising a multicultural festival, it is a good idea to have knowledge of the various cultures being represented. Having just one dressing room may be fine for a local theatre group but does not work for some folk dance groups.

It is a good idea to have a dedicated space for the performers so that they can prepare and rest between performances. This is often called the green room. The green room is also for the hospitality to the artists - i.e. food and drink. In the green room, the various performers' run sheets can be on the walls as well as a copy of the whole production schedule.

It can also provide a place for storage of performers' equipment, the boxes it came in and it is a central place where the artists can be found for interviews or last minute changes.

If the artists are an integral part of the event, then it is a good idea to have an artist liaison person. Their job is to look after the artists when they arrive at the event, while on site and help them leave the event. This job is often left to the stage manger who tends to be busy with other aspects of the staging.

An artist will have technical requirements and these must be well known to the event management. They are often called a "spec sheet" or specifications sheet. It is wise to get this as early as possible as there may be hidden costs. Some acts may have a spec sheet that is over thirty pages long going into great detail such as the model number of the microphone needed. Similar to the spec sheet is the hospitality requirement sheet often called a 'rider'. Once again this should be known as it may have all kinds of implications such as accommodation requirements and accompanying personnel.

Steps and Questions

Look at the performance schedule for the next event and identify where all the performers will be at any given time. Is it wise to have some one liaise with the artists?

Put together the runs sheets for the artist and examine if they can be understood by the artist.

Look at the cultural backgrounds of the artists and examine if this has been taken into account in the event planning.

Conclusion

The heart of many events is the performing artist. He allows the audience the special event experience. In this situation, it is wise to understand as much as possible of the artist, his culture and style of work as possible so that the event - and you - can benefit from a brilliant performance. Correct and fair negotiation combined with respect will achieve that.

APPENDIX F : 10 BIGGEST MISTAKES MOST EVENT PLANNERS MAKE AND HOW TO AVOID THEM

Mistake 1 : FAILING TO IDENTIFY MEETING OBJECTIVES

This is a very common mistake. Be sure to know one hundred percent what your management expects from this meeting. Examples education, recruiting, awards presentations, new product roll-out, awareness etc.

Mistake 2 : FAILING TO BUDGET PROPERLY

Many planners make this mistake by overlooking some very costly items. Specifically travel, audio/visual, programme handouts, shipping charges, decorations, security and afternoon breaks. Don't overlook these costs !

Mistake 3 : FAILING TO SELECT THE RIGHT FACILITY

This mistake can destroy the best event. Things to consider when planning your event

Location, location, location! Depending on the locale of your attendees, proximity to the airport, sleeping room costs, freeways, major thorough fares and traffic patterns are critical. Meeting room location, meeting room size and parking fees, all affect your attendance.

Mistake 4 : FAILING TO HIRE THE RIGHT SPEAKER/ENTERTAINER

Every planner's worst nightmare is a "flop". Be sure to use a reputed, skilled speaker or entertainer whom you have personally seen or whose references you have checked.

Mistake 5 : FAILING TO IDENTIFY AND SECURE A PROSPECT LIST IN ADVANCE.

There are many times when events fail because of this one factor. Secure your entire list before securing your date in writing. Be sure your list has all names, titles, mailing addresses, fax numbers and e-mail addresses. Your attendees can't register if you can't reach them.

Mistake 6 : FAILING TO PREPARE A MARKETING PLAN

This definitely ranks in the top three with regards to importance when learning an event. Be sure to layout your timelines. Get in touch with your contacts by your target dates. Plan your contacts by mail, e-mail, telephone and fax by the week. This will insure maximum contact in a timely manner and will drive your attendance.

Mistake 7 : FAILING TO SECURE STRONG CONTRACTS

Here's where you can really run into trouble. Do NOT promote your event without legible and signed contracts for everything including your speaker, facility, other contractors, entertainer, performer etc.

Mistake 8 : FAILING TO CREATE THE RIGHT ENVIRONMENT

With the hundreds of details we put into every meeting, don't overlook your meeting environment. Lighting, seating, room temperature, music, decorations, audio, visual, location of the bathrooms and telephones are all important.

Mistake 9 : FAILURE TO SECURE THE RIGHT AUDIO/VISUAL

A client spent over Rs. 2,00,000 for audio/visual equipment but the headlining speaker went on stage and looked dumbstruck because the event company had ordered the wrong equipment ! A powerful lesson. Get it in writing! Request a written list of audio/visual needs from every presenter and feed them back to your staging set up.

Mistake 10 : FAILURE TO MARKET THE EVENT PROPERLY

Once you've created your marketing plan, stick to it ! Once your event is booked, it's critical all of your marketing contacts go as planned. Remember; use every means to reach your attendees. One method alone doesn't reach everyone because we are all different. Use every means available to you. Don't forget e-mail and better yet, your sponsors' Good Luck !

| APPENDIX G : SPECIAL EVENT RISK MANAGEMENT |

SPECIAL EVENT RISK MANAGEMENT

It demonstrates the maturity of an industry when it takes an interest in their mistakes, collate them and learn from them. For too long the event industry has ignored the past problems. The trouble arises when there is a major problem which seems to come from nowhere and the results are often devastating. Each event is a unique combination of suppliers, venues, clients, sponsors, audience etc. If we do not learn from our mistakes, as the saying goes, we are condemned to repeat them. The individual event manager certainly can learn from his own mistakes – but this does not make an industry.

Fortunately, the event manager has a tool that can be used for all future events. This is the risk management methodology as set out in project management.

Risk Management

Our industry is based or, risk. By this we mean uncertainty about the future creates risk. An event is a unique combination of elements i.e. suppliers, attendees, clients and therefore has a degree of uncertainty. Most of the event manager's time is spent on reducing that uncertainty. Thy job of risk management is to discover the areas of uncertainty and reduce them. But this alone is not enough for the modem event managers, they must be able to demonstrate how this is done.

The first myth to dispel is that risk management only concerns safety or security. These are important parts of risk management – but they are only parts of it. If the event manager concentrates only on safety issues, then they may miss other areas of risk that impinge on safety. For example, not having enough funds to hire the right number of security staff because a sponsor has pulled out. In this case, the primary risk is the withdrawal of a sponsor.

The secondary risk is the security issues. The advantage event managers have is they are very conscious of safety risk. People are our events. When a person lands on the moon and the world is watching — this makes it a special event — not just an engineering feat. The event manager understands-the basic process to do a full risk management plan. They already do this when they walk the site, looking for problems, such as electrical leads that are not taped down or stairs that are not well lit in white light.

The risk analysis process used is
  - ➢ Identify the risk
  - ➢ Assess the likelihood of the risk occurring
  - ➢ Assess the impact of the risk occurring (severity)
  - ➢ Produce a strategy to practice the risk
  - ➢ Assign the task to practice the risk with a time frame
  - ➢ Monitor the risk
  - ➢ Reassess the risk for further action

It all sounds technical – but if you observe what you do when you ask the caterer for a sample of their food, you are beginning your risk management of this element of the event. Your assessment of the risk may conclude that it is a good idea to take photos of the plate of food so that the caterer knows what you expect on the night of the event, thereby minimising the practihood that they make a mistake at a time when it would be impossible to correct, i.e. just before it is served to the guests.

Hopefully, this example illustrates that the technical risk management process is second nature to the event manager, it is almost intuitive. The next step is to look at all the elements of the event and apply the same process. But there is a problem — how do you identify all these elements? If you leave one out you are not doing a full risk management. This is why risk management is based on project management. The 'elements' are found in the Work Breakdown Structure (WBS). That is, the list of work that needs to be done to get the event practice.

For example, one element of the WBS is sponsorship. A risk in this area may be identified as 'sponsor withdraws from event'. Using the risk analysis process above, we look at the likelihood of it happening and the consequence if it does happen. Then we try to reduce both – if possible. We could reduce the likelihood by making sure that we regularly communicate with the sponsor and understand their business requirements. We can reduce the severity of the consequence by making sure we have other sponsors the take up the slot. What are the other ways the event manager could reduce the risk?

There are more tools and techniques from project management that can be used. These include

1. **Stakeholder Analysis** : Many of the risks arise from the requirements of the stakeholders. Therefore, a stakeholder management plan is a first step in risk management.

2. **Fault Trees :** This technique is used to assist in identifying risk and allow the staff to be consulted and become part of the risk management process. Getting the staff and suppliers involved in risk analysis is an important step.

3. **Documentation :** Proof of risk management is not just an incident free, successful event; it is the documents that recorded the risks and were an integral part of the management of the event. These include incident report sheets and a risk register. They make up the risk management planning document. Such documentation is the basis of project management.

4. **Terminology :** Project risk management gives the event company a list of accurate terms that can describe risk. These are the standards used across all industries. As well the staff has a language to describe the possible problems at the same time as analyse them.

5. **Risk Audit** : The risk audit is related competency and maturity models outlined in the so named conference paper. The aim of the risk audit is to allow the event organisation to know where they are in respect to the standard in the industry. It helps to identify the gaps.

IDENTIFYING RISKS

Identify risks using the following checklist as a prompt.

1. The Organisation

➢ Is the event being run under the auspices of an incorporated organisation?
➢ Has the organising committee been delegated the authority to organise and run the event?
➢ Is the role of the practice committee clear?
➢ Are the responsibilities of the committee members clear?
➢ Is the committee working to established timelines?
➢ Are accurate notes made of proceedings and decisions at meetings?

➢ Is good communication maintained between committee members?
➢ Is good communication maintained between the committee and the parent organisation?
➢ Are practicers aware of their Duty of Care?

2. Finance

➢ Have financial projections been completed to establish the event's viability?
➢ Has finance been allocated as a specific role to a committee member?
➢ Are arrangements in place to segregate event finances from those of the parent organisation?
➢ Are all financial transactions pertaining to the event recorded?
➢ Are receipts kept for all purchases?
➢ Are safeguards in place to protect financial assets?

The above tools and techniques are only a sample of what can be used to assist the event manger to create a risk resilient event organisation.

Conclusion

Risk management planning is increasingly being demanded by event stakeholders such as the government and their agencies, insurance companies, sponsors and the courts. As a practicing event manager, you already know the process and risk management will give you the language to describe it. You can then apply it across the entire event – and even to the strategic aims of your company.

It is vital that the event manager keeps up to date on these issues as well as understands what other industries are doing in risk management.

APPENDIX H : EVENT MANAGEMENT COMPANIES AND EVENT ORGANISERS	
Sr. No.	Event Management Company
1.	A Media Promotions
2.	ABCL
3.	Business FX
4.	Candid Promotions and Action Marketing
5.	Cause Celebre'
6.	Clowns 'R'Us
7.	DNA Networks
8.	Encore
9.	Event Engineers Pvt. Ltd.
10.	Fountainhead
11.	Gold-dust Promotions
12.	Grapevine
13.	Integrated Marketing and Communication Inc.
14.	Kidstuff Promotions

Sr. No.	Event Management Company
15.	Maanz Promotions
16.	Media Entertainment Pvt. Ltd.
17.	Morani
18.	Mudra Diversified
19.	Music Craft
20.	Parnassus
21.	Party Cruisers
22.	Party Liners
23.	Pineapple Club
24.	Pixie Dust
25.	Plus Events
26.	Power Productions
27.	Procam
28.	Professional Management Group
29.	Roger Pereira Communications
30.	Scorpio
31.	Sports Craft
32.	Sportscraft
33.	Stagekraft
34.	Teamwork Films
35.	Trend Setters
36.	Trinity
37.	Tropical Snowflakes
38.	UniRapport Events
39.	Vikram Singh
40.	Vivify
41.	Wizcraft

APPENDIX I : SPONSORS OF THE EVENTS

Sr. No.	Company	Products/Brands	Event Category
1.	BPL	Home Theatre System	Launch Technofesta, Cricket
2.	Coca Cola India	Soft Drinks	Sports, Music, Films, Fests
3.	Reliance	Various	Cricket
4.	Ceat	Tyres	Cricket
5.	Apollo Tyres	Tyres	Cricket, Hot Air Ballooning Expedition
6.	JK Tyres	Tyres	Motor Sports, go-karts

Sr. No.	Company	Products/Brands	Event Category
7.	MRF	Tyres	Cricket
8.	ITC	Tobacco Products	Sports (Classic Polo, Golf, Cricket)
9.	Hero Group	Motor Bikes	Hero Cup
10.	Pepsi	Soft Drinks	Sports, Music, Films, Fests
11.	Jagjit Industries	Various	Sports (Hockey, etc.)
12.	Lakhani Shoes	Shoes	Sports
13.	Action Shoes	Shoes	Sports
14.	Great Glen Distilleries	Liquor	Golf, Tennis
15.	McDonald	Food	Polo, Horse Racing
16.	SAIL	Steel Manufacturing	Football, Cricket
17.	Mahindra & Mahindra	Automobile	Squash
18.	Standard Chartered Bank	Banking	Tennis
19.	Sanghi Group	Various	World Cup Chess
20.	Mesco Shoes	Shoes	Sports with Indian Representation
21.	HLL	Close-up, Lifebuoy & Others	Music, Festivals
22.	Colgate	Dental Care Products	Kite Festivals
23.	TVS	Various	Navratri Festivals
24.	Philips	Consumer Electronics	Fairs & Festivals
25.	Eicher Tractors	Tractors	Fairs & Festivals
26.	Golden Tobacco Company	Cigarettes	Fairs & Festivals
27.	Asian Paints	Paints	Fairs & Festivals
28.	Bayer	Pharmaceutical	Fairs & Festivals
29.	Seagram	Li – uor	Music
30.	American Express	Credit Cards	Martha Graham Dance Show
31.	IDI	Smirnoff Vodka	Special Launches and Co of Event with Ownership
32.	Citibank	Bank	Special Events
33.	Baskin Robbins	Ice Cream	Sports Derby
34.	McDowells	Soda	Sports Derby
35.	Pfizer	Pharmaceuticals	Special Launches
36.	Lee	Jeans	Special Launches

B.B.A. (Semester VI) Examination
EVENT MANAGEMENT
APRIL 2016
(2013 Pattern)

Time : 3 Hours   Max. Marks : 80

N. B. :

(1) *All questions are compulsory.*

(2) *Figures to the right indicate full marks.*

(3) *Draw neat diagrams wherever necessary.*

Q. 1 : Assuming that you are organizing 'A National Level Dance Competition'. As an event manager give an outline for organizing the event. **[15]**

OR

Your college is organizing an intergollegiate quiz competition. Identify the pre-event activities for the same. **[15]**

Q. 2 : What are the criteria for selection of venue ? Explain in-house and external venue. **[15]**

OR

What is event management ? Explain the various functions of event management. **[15]**

Q. 3 : Explain various categories of events along with their characteristics. **[15]**

OR

Describe the basic evaluation process in detail. **[15]**

Q. 4 : Define strategy. Explain the strategic alternatives arising from environmental analysis. **[15]**

OR

Explain in detail the various types of promotion methods used in events. **[15]**

Q. 5 : **Write short notes on (any four) :** **[20]**

  (a) Ambush marketing.

  (b) PREP model.

  (c) Problems associated with traditional media.

  (d) 5 W's of event.

  (e) Revenue generating customers.

  (f) Clients.

www.ingramcontent.com/pod-product-compliance
Lightning Source LLC
Chambersburg PA
CBHW081522050726
47503CB00017B/2871